BATTLE
EARTH XII

NICK S. THOMAS

978-1-911092-26-1

Typeset by Swordworks Books
Printed and bound in the UK & US
A catalogue record of this book is available
from the British Library

Cover design by Swordworks Books
www.swordworks.co.uk

BATTLE
EARTH XII

NICK S. THOMAS

PROLOGUE

For years humanity had fought to protect Earth and her colonies. Millions died fighting the first war against the Alien Lord Karadag. Millions more suffered the same fate against Demiran as humanity faced its second invasion. The forces of Earth fought Demiran to a bitter standstill and finally destroyed his fleet, stranding the aliens' armies on Earth where they could eventually be destroyed.

But that wasn't the end. Erdogan, the most powerful of the Krycenaean Lords, had yet to make his move. And when he did, it came in with brutal and ruthless effectiveness. The power, resources, and tactical prowess of this alien leader made Colonel Mitch Taylor wonder if they had ever made any progress against their technologically advanced and relentless enemy.

All hope for Earth was lost in just a few short weeks of brutal combat. Those who could, fled from the planet in a desperate bid to save humanity. Just three million souls managed to escape the Solar System. Among them the remnants of Colonel Taylor's Inter-Allied Regiment.

With dwindling resources, and an ever-present risk of pursuit by the enemy, the most unlikely of encounters occurred. Another race was discovered - The Aranui. A race more advanced than both human and Krycenaean, but with fewer than one thousand population. The threat of Erdogan eventually forced humans and Aranui into an alliance against their common enemy.

Access to advanced technologies seemed to give hope of taking Earth back from Erdogan and his vast armies. A first mission to Earth proved successful, but when Taylor learnt of Commander Kelly's capture by enemy forces, he was compelled to act. A successful rescue attempt appeared to pave the way for victory, until a horrifying fact was revealed in a bloodthirsty fashion. Kelly and the hundreds of soldiers rescued from Earth were not who they appeared to be, but were enemy clones. Taylor had been deceived and paid a dear price.

Eli Parker died before his eyes, and many more of his comrades fell as the clones were revealed and butchered them, including the Admiral of the fleet and his command staff. The clones were defeated, but not before inflicting a crippling blow to those who thought they had escaped Erdogan's reach.

It was clear to Taylor that there was only one way the

war could be ended - kill Erdogan, and he was willing to sacrifice anything he had to achieve that goal.

CHAPTER ONE

"You ready to kick some ass?" Silva screamed.

The marines all around him roared with enthusiasm to have their blood lust fulfilled.

"Are you ready to wade in rivers of blue blood?"

The volume only increased as the Sergeant Major psyched them up for combat. He looked around and smiled as he could feel the atmosphere was thick with enthusiasm. There were just twenty-five marines aboard the Eagle assault copter, but their response in the confined space was electric. He closed his eyes for just a few seconds and listened to the enthusiastic cheers echo in his eardrums. For just a moment he could suspend reality and imagine he was at a stadium before a big game. Then he opened his eyes once again and caught sight of Colonel Taylor.

The Colonel's face was deadly serious. He seemed to stare into the distance in complete concentration or a daze. Either way he was in his own world and appeared to have missed everything Silva had said. He was a different man since Eli Parker's death, and that was plain for all to see. Light flooded in through the cockpit as they passed through the atmosphere and into a gleaming bright blue sky.

"Hey, Colonel!"

There was no way Taylor could not have heard the roar of Silva's voice, but he seemed so distant it didn't seem that he was deliberately ignoring him. Even so, it was a worry for Silva, as he needed to know he could rely on their leader. He pushed his way through two marines to stand in front of him. He slapped one hand down on his shoulder hard enough that it forced Taylor to turn slightly and take note of him. He glared at him as if to burn him for daring to put a hand on him. But Silva still wasn't sure if that was scorn or merely a vague blankness.

"A distracted marine..."

He waited for Taylor to finish his sentence, but the response never came.

"Is a dead marine," he added.

Taylor made no sign of acknowledgement at all.

"Come on, Colonel, give me something. I need to know your head is in this, in the right place."

Taylor slowly shook his head.

"This is the only place I have left," he replied, "All I have is the need to fight. I am not distracted. I am more focused than I ever have been."

The statement took Silva back and scared him a little. He could see Taylor had become a little unhinged. It reminded him of Jones after he had come back to them from being a captive of the enemy, but he dared not say so.

"ETA two minutes!" Rains called out.

Taylor nodded in acknowledgement and turned back to his marines. His platoon leader Lieutenant Matthews stood beside him and Captain Morris. The former MDF officer had struggled to find his place amongst the Inter-Allied, and finally settled as Taylor's number two. He never strayed far from the Colonel, and Taylor was comfortable with that. It was proof that he had at least saved one of Kelly's people. The two Germans, Sergeant Lang and Private Fuchs were behind him. They had become hardened veterans and long earned the right to call themselves part of the Regiment. Corporal Herrera pushed his way forward to better hear what Taylor was about to say, his hand never leaving the grab handle bar above them.

"Still alive, Corporal?" Taylor asked.

"Somebody has to watch your back," he replied.

Taylor nodded. With so many faces having changed over the years, it was good to have marines like him and Silva still at his side. All of them looked weary. It was hard to tell if it was through lack of sleep or a general weariness of war, perhaps both. Taylor could see they would be a hard crowd to get excited about anything, and that made Silva's achievements all the more impressive.

"We hit this facility and we seriously hamper the enemy's ability to repair their aircraft. Air superiority isn't something we have seen in a long time, and taking this place down is a good step towards getting it back! We've hit their supply lines, and we've hit their convoys and patrols. Now it's time to hit a little harder! When we get down there, I want to see nothing short of complete and utter annihilation of any Mech bastard you find. However many shots you think you need to bring one down, you double it. Double up on charges to destroy vital targets. Stab those fuckers until they are sawn in two! No mercy, let's make them pay for ever dreaming they could have our land!"

The marines roared with excitement, all but Jafar who loomed over them at the back of the copter. He was carrying so many explosive charges on his armour that he looked almost twice his regular size. Taylor nodded to acknowledge him, and he returned the gesture, though he didn't seem to possess the level of excitement and blood lust the others did.

"Thirty seconds!" yelled Rains.

They felt the reverse thrusters kick in and bring them to a halt in what seemed to be almost instantaneous.

"Go, go, go!" cried Rains.

The doors either side of the craft slid open, and Taylor leapt up without a word and before anyone else could move. He went forward with such determination it was an inspiration to all that went after him. As Taylor hit the ground, a pulse landed just a metre away from his feet, and he knew they were in for a hard fight. He raised his shield in front of him, and another shot glanced off the thick armour. He quickly scanned the area for targets and could see fire coming from a tower up ahead. He started advancing and laying down cover fire when a beam struck the tower, and it was engulfed in flames. He turned to see two of the Guardians had landed just thirty metres to his flank.

"Hell, yeah!" Herrera shouted as they celebrated the immense destructive firepower of their allies' weapons.

God help us if we ever have to fight them again, Taylor thought.

He turned back to the fight and rushed forward to the cover of some sort of maintenance vehicle that was five metres long and taller than he stood. He smashed into the flank of the heavy vehicle as pulses landed around him, and Morris staggered and rolled up beside him.

"Thought this was going to be easy?"

"What gave you that impression?"

Morris shrugged. "You made it sound like a walk in the park."

"Compared to some of the shit we've been through, yeah."

Several pulses smashed into the vehicle above them and sent splashes of the burning hot material spraying close over their heads. They quickly ducked down a little lower.

"Is that what we measure things by now? How much better they were than the shittiest times?"

"Seems reasonable," replied Taylor as more pulses smashed into the vehicle at their backs.

Morris couldn't tell if he was joking or not, so he just shook his head. Taylor got up and peered through a head size hole that had been ripped through the upper skin of the vehicle. It provided a convenient loophole from which to survey the enemy positions up ahead. He could see gunfire coming from the slit in the side of a building that was clearly a well-concealed bunker. But before he could say a word, he heard Silva shouting and turned to see dozens of Mech pilots rushing for the craft lined up to their flank.

"Don't let them get to the ships!"

Taylor raised his rifle and took aim. With his first burst he killed one outright and fire began to pour into them, but many made it into the cover of their craft.

"Shit!"

Just as he cursed, one of their own craft dropped in low, and a Guardian leapt from it at a height of almost twenty metres. The huge UAV Mech landed dead on the cockpit of one of the enemy craft, crushing the pilot in the process. It was upright and firing just a second after landing, and Taylor watched in amazement as the Guardian blasted the craft and the crews apart before they could get off the ground. A few of the pilots tried to scatter, and Taylor was quick to shoot them down before they could reach cover. Morris couldn't bring himself to pull the trigger.

"It's a turkey shoot," he muttered.

"Yeah? Well best make the most of it," replied Taylor.

Morris raised his gun and took aim at one of the pilots, but he hesitated, and Taylor fired three shots into his target before he could make a decision.

"You lost your stomach for this or what?" Taylor asked him furiously.

"I've just been on the other end of this, and I prayed for mercy and an end to it. I can't do it."

He looked at Taylor as if expecting him to agree and accept his statement, but instead Taylor punched him in the face. The strike wasn't full force, but it was enough to take him off balance, as much by force as surprise, and he toppled over to the ground. Taylor rushed over to him and forced his knee onto Morris' throat so that he was pinned down.

"You hesitate and marines die. You start feeling for the enemy and marines die. You do anything but your job, and that is killing Mechs, and you will cause marines to die. You let that happen, and I'll shoot you myself."

Morris was shocked by his words, and in that moment

realised what a different man Taylor had become. He wasn't just angry and at a loss, he was entirely engulfed with a rage that would have him do nothing else but kill.

"What'll it be? Will you do your job, or do I have to relieve you of your duties?"

Morris finally nodded in agreement. Taylor got off him and offered him his hand before hauling him to his feet.

"No time in this war for compassion. Save that for when it's over," added Taylor.

He went back to the cover of the vehicle and took aim at targets further into the base. Silva moved up beside Morris, and the Captain looked to him for answers.

"Colonel's right," said Silva.

Morris stopped him and grabbed his arm.

"When this is all over, we're gonna have to live with those aliens, you know that, right?"

Silva shook his head. "We don't know what the hell's gonna happen. But imagining a world where we have won this war is a luxury we can't afford right now, and it won't ever happen while we piss about discussing the possibility." He shrugged off Morris' hand and carried on to Taylor's side.

"King should be here by now!" said Silva.

"Yeah, well he ain't," Taylor said and activated his comms.

"Anders, push that left flank. Robinson, see if you can't breach that bunker."

A salvo of pulses smashed into one of the Guardians. It was damaged in multiple areas and was forced to take cover behind a small hangar building where another joined it.

"Little more resistance that you expected?"

"Nope, Sergeant, just about right. Facility like this was never gonna be an easy take," replied Taylor.

He looked around the corner of the vehicle and fired a few shots for suppression, but he couldn't make out much of a target. As he did so, he noticed another bunker encased in a building as the other had been, and multiple pulses flashed towards him from its location. He was forced to duck back down for cover. Taylor looked over to Robinson's platoon to see they were deploying both a pig for suppressing fire and an AT launcher.

"Think it'll go through that?" Silva asked.

"We can only hope."

They watched as the launcher was fired and the high velocity explosive charge rushed towards the first bunker. It went right through one of the vision slits and exploded. The eruption shook the ground beneath them. The front of the bunker was blown off, and part of the building above it collapsed to the ground, burying whoever was still alive inside. Cheers rang out, but just a split second later a burst of pulse fire struck the man who had fire the AT launcher. His loader hauled him back into cover, and their celebrations were immediately halted.

17

"Fuck!" Taylor yelled.

He simply couldn't contain himself as he watched the wounded marine being hauled into cover, and his prospects didn't look good. As a medic reached him, the loader went right back to the weapon, put in a charge, and took aim at the second bunker. She lifted the device onto her shoulder and squeezed the trigger. They all watched with anticipation as the shot soared towards the defences but impacted on the surface. The explosion sent a burst of debris and dust out in front of the bunker, but it soon settled and showed only minimal damage.

They all watched in amazement as the woman continued to load another shot, but as she did so, a pulse struck the launcher itself and it burst in two. The medic reached forward and hauled her into cover just before a salvo of fire struck the place where she had been standing just moments before. Then they heard the most horrible of sounds; the rapid fire anti-aircraft Mech weaponry that was like a Gatling gun going off. The shots were coming from behind the bunker positions, and they looked up just in time to see one of their own copters burst into flames and plunge into a nearby hangar.

Every one of them wondered if the craft had still been carrying its quota of marines, but they didn't want to imagine the worst-case scenario.

"Ours?" Morris asked.

Silva shook his head.

"That's one of Moye's."

"Poor bastards."

Captain King finally came over on the comms.

"This is Taylor, where the hell are you?"

"Our bird took a hit. We made it to the ground, but we landed right in the shit. Looks like some kind of barracks, and we're up to our fucking necks in Mech soldiers."

"And the rest of your Company?"

"Down here with me trying to dig ourselves out of this mess. We ain't gonna be getting to you anytime soon, Colonel. I'm sorry."

Taylor shook his head and turned to see a number of the French copters turning back.

"Guess we're it?" Silva asked, "Some things never change."

Taylor surveyed the scene once again and could now see several other elevated positions beyond the first bunker that were starting to lay down fire. All around he could see his people dug in to any cover they could find. Even the three Guardians could not move for fear of being blasted by heavy pulse fire.

"We gotta take down those AA guns or we ain't getting any more help."

"Easier said than done," added Silva.

With that, Taylor rushed out from cover. He accelerated to a sprinting speed within a few short paces, and then leapt twenty metres into the air using his booster and above the line of fire that landed all around him. The rest of the unit could do nothing but watch in amazement as their commander soared through the air. The few enemy that could, returned fire but could not find their target due to the speed he travelled at. He landed down before the second bunker and hit the ground running.

"What on earth is he doing, Sergeant?" Morris asked.

"Kicking some fucking ass."

Taylor slammed into the side of the bunker and dropped his rifle to let it hang by his side. He drew out two grenades, primed them, and tossed them through the slit, ducking back for cover. A moment later an explosion rang out, and a metre-wide hole blasted out from the front of the bunker. Before the dust had settled, Taylor had put the muzzle of his rifle into the breach and opened up on full auto. He emptied an entire magazine before ducking back and reloading, and beckoning for the others to join him.

Without hesitation, the three platoons arose from cover and rushed out across the open ground. With shields held before them, they took pulse after pulse. The heavier pulse cannons cut two of them down, but the rest covered the ground quickly. Soon Silva and Morris were up against the wall of the bunker next to Taylor, just as they had been before.

"You're crazy, you know that? And we love you for it," Silva said with a smile, but Taylor still looked deadly serious. He looked at his watch and sighed.

"This is taking too long. Another ten minutes and they'll be on top of us, and then we're fucked."

Neither of them could disagree, but neither did it make it any less crazy. They watched the heavy weapons teams bring up the cumbersome machine guns that they'd need before an advance.

"Get those weapons firing!" Taylor ordered.

The crews were taking fire and struggling to get set up, but Taylor yelled at them once again.

"Move it, move it! We're running out of time!"

He turned back. Silva was looking at him with an appalled expression on his face.

"You got a problem, Sergeant Major?"

"Pushing everyone a little hard, aren't you, Sir? This lots luck can't last forever."

"Luck is for those who don't have skill or a will to get the job done. I expect more."

"More than what?"

"More than yesterday, more than they have done before, more…everything."

Silva didn't know how to respond, so he didn't.

"I don't see why we are still pushing this," muttered Morris, "We've already smashed their air power here. Look at them," he said, pointing at the craft the Guardians had torn apart and the dozens of bodies they had left in their wake.

"You know there's plenty more below the surface," said

Silva.

"No, we think there are. We don't know for sure either way. Has anyone seen them?"

"We'll know soon enough."

"Or we'll die trying to find out."

"Sir, you are out of line," said Silva.

Morris was silenced for a moment but finally replied, "How dare you! I am an officer in this Regiment…" he went on, but was soon interrupted by Taylor.

"Shut the fuck up!"

Morris was so shocked and intimidated by Taylor that he did as he was told and waited for the Colonel to continue.

"You all know the deal. Intel says there's at least double their number beneath our feet. I won't go until we either destroy what they've got or confirm it ain't there. Got it?"

Morris nodded in agreement. It was plain for all to see that Taylor was a changed man. He was as capable as ever, but so much of his humour and friendship qualities were gone. Silva could see he had turned into an efficient machine, and whilst that got the job done, it was disconcerting from the man he had known as a friend and leader for so many years.

Taylor looked over to the Guardians, and they too were waiting for his orders. He looked back at his watch once more and knew that time was against them.

"If we don't move in the next thirty seconds, we might as well turn our backs and run. Run and leave a great opportunity. So we've taken out a couple of dozen Mech craft? What if we could destroy another hundred? We're either in this to win or not. Are you with me?"

Silva nodded in agreement without hesitation, and Morris soon followed. Taylor quickly turned and simply yelled one word. "Charge!"

It was all he needed to say, as everybody knew their part. A dozen of the marines managed to get ahead before Taylor could get out from the cover of the rubble of the bunker. He held his shield out before him as pulses crashed over the defence it provided, and he went forward without any fear at all.

Taylor fired as he went, but he couldn't find a target worth aiming at. He then found a wall for defence and pushed up against it. He was followed by many of his marines who waited for his next move. There was only one entrance leading through the two metre high walls.

"We aren't going through there," stated Silva.

Taylor agreed. "Only a fool would. We'll go over."

He went a few metres back, and then used the last of the power in his boosters to launch him up and over the wall. As he descended, he found he was coming back down on top of a dozen Mechs. Mitch put his shield under him and felt the impact of several pulses beneath him, finally landing on one of the enemy soldiers and crushing it to the ground.

He rolled off the Mech and raised his shield over

him just in time to absorb a pulse that burst across the surface as he held it out. Gunfire rang out seconds later. The descending marines hit the Mechs around him by a hail of gunfire. A Mech standing over him spasmed, hit in the back by several shots from Reitech rifles. Taylor took his opportunity to rise up and draw his Assegai, driving it deep into the creature's abdomen.

As the creature fell down dead, he could feel his blood lust grow, until Jafar dropped in next to him, and he realised the shots had come from his alien friend. He wanted to say thanks but couldn't bring himself to do it, and Jafar never required it. Mitch was back on his feet now and rushing towards the next Mech. He shield barged the beast and then thrust his Assegai into its neck as it stumbled backwards.

Taylor pushed ahead even as his comrades were still battling the creatures all around him. He could see the anti-aircraft emplacements now. Each of the four dome shaped towers had six barrels protruding from their thickly armoured roofs. At the base of the first were two guards already fixing their weapons on him, but Taylor fired first and Silva joined him. The two creatures were cut down before getting off a shot, and he could see another inside trying to shut the hinged blast door at the base of the tower. Taylor sped up and stormed towards the door.

Just as the door was about to connect with its frame, the edge of his shield connected with its centre. With his entire body weight behind him, he barrelled in through the entrance and landed on top of another creature. Silva was through the door a second later and fired a burst from his rifle into the one who had been attempting to shut them out. Taylor thrust his Assegai into the head of the one he was sprawled across.

"What now?" Silva asked.

Jafar rushed through the doorway behind them as Taylor got to his feet.

"You think you can control these guns?" Taylor asked him.

Jafar simply nodded and stepped into an open frame elevator as if intimately familiar with the construction. Taylor and Silva stepped in beside him and it was all the space there was. Jafar hit a button, and they rocketed up at a surprising rate until finally slowing. They found they had reached the gunnery deck. Three aliens sat at consoles and simply stared in shock at their presence. Nobody moved for a second. Taylor lifted his rifle and fired three shots into the chest of the middle one.

The other two aliens leapt out of their seats to reach for guns on a rack beside them, but it was too late. Silva and Jafar opened fire on both of them, and blood was splashed across the consoles as they dropped down dead.

"Well?" Taylor asked, "Can you bring these guns to bear on the other towers?"

Jafar pushed one of the bodies aside and took a seat.

They watched the huge screen displaying the view from the gun ports. He took aim at the first tower and squeezed the triggers on the joysticks either side of him. Light flashed before their eyes, and the first tower was obliterated in a few short seconds. Jafar immediately brought the guns around to target the next tower and could see them both rotating to engage them.

"Oh, shit," Silva swore under his breath.

"Get a shift on!" Taylor yelled.

He opened fire and strafed the first from top to bottom until it began to topple, finally collapsing into the last of the towers still opposing them. Silva gave out a sigh of relief as he realised they had been just seconds from certain death.

"Not bad," said Taylor, patting Jafar on the shoulder, "We can't leave this place standing," he added.

He drew out a grenade and set a ninety-second timer and placed it on the console beside Jafar. Silva placed two others, and they made their way quickly to the elevator and headed for the door. As they walked out into the light of day, Captain King and his Rangers met them, approaching from the north. They looked like they'd been through a hard fight, but King had a smile on his face, despite the blood trickling down his face.

"You made it at last, then?"

"Didn't exactly go to plan, Colonel, but we sure got a few bonus kills on the way."

As he finished, the grenades in the tower ignited. One of the gun barrels broke loose from the tower and smashed down to the ground a metre from Taylor's feet. He looked up with disgust to see the thickly armoured structure still stood in defiance.

"It'll have to do. At least we've rendered it useless," he stated to Silva.

He looked around to see that all eyes were on him now.

"Intel told us what's on the surface is just the very tip of the iceberg, so let's find out!"

As he said it, they heard the sound of engines roaring beneath them and looked back. A kilometre away the guns of the Diderot opened fire as two Mech fighters burst out from the mountainside a few hundred metres from her.

"Guess we just found the entrance to their landing strip," said King.

They watched as the Diderot first hammered the two craft with close range weaponry before the big guns finally opened up on the entrance to the underground hangar. The echoes of the guns sounded like a thunderstorm and brought a smile to Taylor's face.

"All right, the hole is plugged. Time to finish this."

He carried on to a large set of blast doors. They clearly led into the facility, and he pointed for the Guardians to get to work. They immediately hit the opening of the doors and began cutting through. Thirty seconds later they stopped firing, and one of them rushed at the damaged opening, smashing into it with all its force. The doorway partly buckled, and another then joined it and prised the doorway open. Half a metre was all they could get it apart.

"It'll do!" Taylor said.

He held his shield before him as if expecting to be shot at any second, but as he continued to advance, there was nothing. He stood next to the two Guardians who were too large to fit through the breach. He looked at his watch again, noting just how short on time they were.

"Bring up the nuke!" he barked.

He pointed for Sergeant Lang to go through with him, and a second later he darted forward and went through the breach. To their surprise, they found no sign of the enemy at all. All that was there was a large elevator like you'd find on an aircraft carrier.

"We don't have time to go down there," said Silva.

"We don't need to. Bring up that nuke!"

One of the marines strode in with a large steel box on the back of his Reitech suit.

"Right there," said Taylor, pointing to the centre of the elevator.

Two others came up beside him and unclipped the device from his suit and lowered it carefully to the deck.

"Arm it, five minute timer."

"Five minutes?" asked Silva. He sounded shocked, "Cutting it a little fine, don't you think?"

"Do it," he said and opened a comms channel.

"Rains, get your ass down here. I want pickup at our primary extractions in two minutes!"

"You got it, Colonel," Rains answered calmly.

They set up the timer on the nuke and waited for Taylor to activate it. He stepped up and quickly punched in the eight-digit code onto the keypad without any hesitation at all. He looked over to Jafar and nodded for him to activate the huge elevator as they all stepped off. It jolted into action at a slow pace but began to accelerate quickly. Taylor leaned out of the exposed edge to see it drop about thirty metres below the surface and finally come to a halt. He took a step back, targeted a control box and cabling on the far side, and opened fire.

"Rip it apart!" he yelled.

A dozen of the marines around him fired, and Jafar blew out the control module he had used to lower the elevator down.

"Right, let's get the hell out of here!"

He rushed to the smashed doorway and waited for the last of them to go before stepping back out into the light himself.

"It's done?" King asked.

Taylor didn't break stride as he rushed past the Captain.

"Yeah, we've got four minutes till she blows.

"Four minutes? Are you fucking kidding me?"

"You better believe it," added Silva as he ran past him.

"Let's go, go, go!" yelled King to his Company.

The two Companies rushed back over the ground they had fought hard to secure and could see the copters coming in to land nearby.

"Could have given us a little more leeway, Colonel!" Silva shouted breathlessly.

"Just keep moving!"

They jumped aboard the copters and were in the air with just two minutes to spare.

"We've got incoming!" Rains shouted.

Taylor rushed to the cockpit and could see enemy craft approaching on the scanners.

"Can you make it to the Diderot?"

"Probably, but it's gonna be awfully tight."

"The craft soared towards the French Heavy Cruiser that was engaging several of the enemy ships a few kilometres out and couldn't have been more than a couple of thousand feet above the surface.

Then the docking bays were in sight, and Rains barely seemed to slow down as they came crashing into land. The undercarriage hit hard, and they felt part of it buckle as they listed over and ground to a halt. Sparks flew up around them and caused the copter to make a one hundred and eighty degree turn. Its tail struck one of the other copters that had landed moments before. As the loading bay ramps began to close, they could see enemy craft on the horizon.

Taylor looked down to his watch and could see the

countdown was on just five seconds. He hit the comms channel and yelled, "All aboard, go!"

The engines were already spooled up and ready to go. They caught a glimpse of light as the nuke went off, and they vanished into the self-generated space gateway a split second later. Nobody said a word for a moment until Rains started to laugh. It was incongruous, but so many of the others couldn't help but join in.

CHAPTER TWO

Only a few hours had passed since their assault on a military installation on Earth, and Taylor was once again descending to the surface of Onekaka, or as it was now affectionately known as 'Ony'.

"Bet Rains will be coddling that copter for hours, trying to iron out all the damage," said Silva humorously, but that was lost on Taylor who simply replied, "Good, we need it operational again ASAP."

The shuttle carrying them was one that used to do runs between the Lunar colony and Earth and had a capacity of one hundred. Windows allowed everyone aboard to see out, and it had no weapons or armour to speak of at all.

"You must have travelled in this girl more than a few times?" Silva asked Morris.

He shook his head.

"I rarely ever had a reason to go to Earth before the

wars."

Silva shook his head.

"What is it?" Morris asked.

"Well, I am with the Colonel on this. I can't see why any human would want to spend their lives entirely in environmentally controlled confines with such a harsh environment outside. Wouldn't you be climbing the walls to get to some real air? Didn't you ever want to just walk on grass and rocks and enjoy all that nature has to offer?"

Morris smiled.

"You were born on Earth, so I guess it's natural you like it. To me it's just an area with too many uncertainties and variables, the weather and temperatures and constantly changing. It's hard work getting anything done when you're contending with all that."

"So you'd go right back to the Moon if you could?"

Morris nodded slowly and let his mind slip back into a time when he still lived there. They were entering the atmosphere of Ony now with several other transports and two of the Aranui vessels who had gone in support of them. The second they had put down on the surface, Taylor was already at the door and storming out as quickly as he could, but he was soon stopped in his tracks by Major Moye.

"Glad to see you made it, Colonel. Got an official casualty list yet?"

Taylor shook his head. It was clear to them all he hadn't

given their losses a second thought, and yet he didn't regret it.

"You must have done okay," he replied, "We didn't see any ground reinforcements beyond the shit King landed in the middle of."

"We paid a heavy price protecting your asses," Moye replied sternly.

"Yeah, price ain't all paid yet," said Taylor, seemingly without any sympathy at all as he carried on walking past the Major. Moye turned and walked with him.

"I hate to bring this up, Colonel, but we need more recruits. We're not getting volunteers in numbers fast enough right now."

"What do you want me to do about it?"

"Admiral Lasure is in charge of the fleet now, but you put him there. You have a lot of say in how things go on around here."

"Talk bluntly, Major, what do you want me to do?"

"Get the Admiral to begin conscription."

Taylor stopped dead in his tracks.

"You know how long it's been since any civilised country on Earth has done that?"

"But we aren't on Earth, and neither are we a country. We're an army and a navy with a lot of civilians hanging on."

Taylor sighed and thought about it for a moment.

"You know the dangers of lowering the quality of the

average fighting man when you bring that to the table?"

"I didn't say I wanted to do it, Colonel. I say we have to do it. If we don't win this, then they're dead anyway."

Taylor slowly nodded his head and looked back to Silva.

"Have them ready for 0600 tomorrow, same as before."

"Getting into a bit of a pattern, aren't we?"

"Yes, Major, a pattern of taking Erdogan's forces down piece-by-piece, and he must be feeling it by now," added Taylor.

Silva began barking his orders at the troops still disembarking from the transport. Taylor finally looked back to Moye and could see he wasn't going to take no for an answer.

"I'll see what I can do. Walk with me."

Taylor carried onwards, but his first stop was to an ammo dump en route to HQ. He walked in to find a quartermaster arguing with a Lieutenant, but on seeing Taylor, they both fell silent until the quartermaster finally asked.

"What can I get you, Colonel?"

Taylor pulled out six empty magazines from his webbing and threw them down on the counter.

"Six mags and three HE grenades."

"You got it, Colonel."

Everything he had asked for was placed before him in a matter of seconds. Taylor loaded up his webbing and smiled at the frustrated Lieutenant before walking back out.

"You know with the role you have taken around here, you can do more good than just what you do with your own hands. After all, you are only one man, one marine. But as a leader you can do so much more."

"I'm doing what I can, but if you think I'm ever gonna be caught unprepared again, you don't know me at all."

Taylor stopped and put a hand in the way of Moye and looked down at his lack of armour. All he carried was a sidearm.

"Mechs attack, right now? Clones reveal themselves? One of the Aranui decides they got a beef with you? What are you gonna do about it? Expect everyone else to do the fighting for you?"

"Sometimes a leader must take a backseat and command."

"Yeah, and that's no excuse for complacency."

"Colonel, I am not some paper pusher who has never had to get his hands dirty. You of all people know that."

"Yes, you're a good fighter, Major, but you're a fighter first and a leader second. And until such time that someone pins stars on your uniform, you'd do well to remember that."

Moye thought on his words for a moment, and Taylor turned and carried onwards as Captain Morris joined them.

"Captain, I have the Sergeant Major preparing the

Regiment for our next operation. You'd do well to be sure you're ready also."

"I'm good to go," he replied confidently.

Taylor looked over to see he was clutching a pile of fresh magazines and grenades that he was stuffing into his webbing. It brought a small smile to Taylor's face that the Captain was following his lead.

"You see, Major, a man who is always ready."

They carried on to the HQ building that had been established and directly into the operations room, where they found twenty officers and other staff busy at work. In the middle of the room sat General White. He was perched in a wheelchair and looked both exhausted and unwell.

"Well done," he said on seeing the two of them, "That was a vital military installation destroyed and with acceptable losses."

Taylor grimaced at the term 'acceptable'. It never sat well with him.

"We got the job done, Sir."

White beckoned for them to come closer, so he could talk with a little more privacy. He took in a deep breath, and it was clear he needed to get something heavy off his chest.

"Taylor, you know I am in a bad way. My wounds are recovering slowly, some of them maybe not at all. I'm old."

"You've got some fight left in you yet, Sir."

White nodded in appreciation as he went on.

"You've taken on a much bigger role around here than your rank would suggest, Colonel..."

Taylor thought he could see where this was going and quickly interrupted.

"I'm not looking for promotion, General, and I don't want it either."

White shook his head. "No, I didn't imagine that you did. You're already spending most of your time doing the duties of a Captain or Major at most. Hell, the only reason you have the rank of Colonel is so that you can lead your own unit, and yet you've taken it upon yourself to make some big decisions. You somehow promoted a Captain to the Admiral of the fleet, making him superior to all of us. And the craziest thing of all is that everyone has accepted it."

"It was necessary, Sir," Taylor spat back.

White seemed shocked by his response.

"It was not a criticism, Colonel. For what it's worth, I think Lasure has already shown himself to be well up to the task. My point, Colonel, is that you are making decisions a Colonel should never make."

"Well, you've got me, Sir. I did, and here we are."

White nodded in agreement.

"Let's be clear. My body is a wreck. I may yet one day recover, but at present I am unable to fulfil my duties as a General in the United States Marine Corps. Hell, I'm not sure the Corps even exists anymore. Most of your Regiment are from other services or even other nations."

"It exists if we say it does, and we keep fighting for it," said Taylor confidently.

White seemed impressed with his commitment.

"I'll stay on here, doing what I can, but I cannot be considered much more than an advisor right now. The command structure is in tatters. We've got officers from a few dozen different nations pushing for their bit of power, and then we have you, Colonel, the man that is holding it all together. Lasure has been accepted as Admiral because you put him there, and there is not one among us in this fleet that would dare question that decision."

Taylor was speechless. He'd never given it so much thought.

"That's a lot of responsibility for a Colonel. Hell, that's a lot of responsibility for one man. While you remain alive, and keep doing what you've been doing, you have the undying support of this fleet. Remember that. You are accepted by mob rule, and the voice of the mob can be more powerful than you can imagine. You keep doing right by them and you're safe. Veer off that path, and you could find a rope around your neck."

"There is only one task I must fulfil, only one thing left in this world I must achieve. Kill that son of a bitch Erdogan. I will find him, and I will kill him. I don't care how long it takes and what price I have to pay. This will end with me tearing his head off and holding up high for all his armies to see."

"And I don't know a single man or woman who wouldn't do all in their power to see you reach that day."

Taylor could see it was his opportunity.

"If the civilians are as committed to this action as we are, then we need them to join this fight, Sir."

"We've been bringing plenty of them into the fold. We've got training camps running night and day to get recruits in the field."

"We need more," stated Taylor.

"We need conscription," Moye said from behind him.

White was shocked by the concept and had to think about it for a few moments.

"I can't ask that of them."

"You don't ask for conscription, General," added Moye, "You order it."

White shook his head. "I have already said I am but an advisor here. The Admiral would have the say on this matter, and even beyond him, he may not have the sway to bring over a few of the nations. You know how many Generals we have in this fleet?"

Taylor shook his head.

"Last count was thirty-four. Half of them were in this room just an hour ago. They will all expect a say on what happens to their own nation's people."

"I don't believe we have that divide anymore," said Taylor, "We aren't Americans, or French, or British. We're one now."

"Try telling that to them. If you want to call up civilians without their volunteering, the only one that can stand a chance of achieving it is you. Any one of us tries it, and we'll be shot down in flames. We could have another mutiny on our hands. Maybe you'd call it civil war now. You can ask it, Taylor, only you."

Taylor shook his head. The responsibilities were piling up on top of him, and he was feeling swamped and stifled by it all. He turned and looked to Moye, but he only nodded in agreement with what the General had said.

"I think you are starting to understand now, Taylor. You're too important to lose, but neither can we take you out of harm's way, as you are vital to the war effort."

"So don't die," said Moye.

"Yeah, thanks."

"So what'll it be?" White asked.

"If we're gonna do this, I'll have to go through Lasure first."

"He'll accept whatever decision you make," said White.

"Maybe, but that is not how we do this. Get me a line to the Admiral."

White didn't hesitate to press a few buttons on the console before him. Taylor's head spun while he considered how he could broach such a subject to the civilian population of the fleet. Twenty seconds later he was shaken by Moye; he had gone into a daze and forgotten everything that was around him.

"What can I do for you, Colonel?" Lasure was now projected before them.

"Admiral. Major Moye here believes we are not getting enough volunteers, and that conscription is necessary if we are to keep up a sustainable force for our attacks on Earth."

Lasure was even more shocked than White had been.

"What do you think, General?" Lasure asked.

"It doesn't matter what I think. This is a numbers game. They have more. We've got tens of thousands of military personnel fighting for our survival, and we've got probably hundreds of thousands of fit and able civilians who would be able to fight."

"And you need my authority to issue such an edict? You know if I do this we could have full-scale riots, mutinies, and unrest on our hands? It's not just about those civilians. How do you think our crews will feel having their families and loved ones asked to go to war?"

"I think they'd understand by now," replied Taylor quickly.

Lasure laughed. "Understand? Plenty of people haven't been all that understanding of my sudden promotion. How do you think it would go down if I tried this? I could be deposed within a day."

"Then don't."

Lasure looked confused by the General's response.

"The Colonel here is our poster boy. Let him take it to them. He gets shot down for it, and we carry on as is. They accept it, and you pass the edict without any problems. You can't lose on this one, Admiral."

Lasure thought for a moment, then turned his attention back to Taylor.

"And you're happy doing this? Happy forcing civilians into this fight?"

"They seem happy to let us fight and die for them, so yes. Every fit man and woman not in a protected profession should already have signed up. But if they haven't, then we'll have to give them a bit of a push."

"And you think they'll go along with being forced?"

"Maybe forcing them isn't the way, but shaming them? What if I could make those people suitable actually want to come forward and sign up?"

"I don't see how. They've lost so much. Wanting to go and fight such a vicious enemy does not sound appealing."

"You leave that to me. Get me an open line to everyone in this fleet. I mean everywhere. Every ship, shuttle, and screen that exists."

"That's not a problem; a priority broadcast can be initiated in ten seconds with my authorisation."

"Then do it, Admiral."

"Right now?"

Taylor nodded.

"Seven missions in seven days, Colonel, don't you think some rest and time to prep this might be a good idea?"

"Yes it would, General, but if time were on our side, we'd do a great many things differently."

White couldn't disagree.

"You will be live with the fleet in five seconds, Colonel," said Lasure.

Taylor looked to the screen to see a countdown. He expected his pulse to rise as the pressure mounted, but he felt nothing. He watched it count down to three…two… one. The screen simply displayed how he looked to all that would be seeing him on screens, and a message at the top of the screen that read 'live' in red letters. There were no prompts at all until Moye finally nudged him in the back. He coughed to clear his throat and righted his posture before looking dead centre into the screen.

"I am Colonel Mitch Taylor of the Inter-Allied Regiment. I am here for just one reason, so please hear me out. Over the last few years I have seen those serving with and beside me achieve incredible results, but at a phenomenal price. I think probably three quarters of the friends I had before we encountered alien life have now lost their lives. For those out there not currently serving in the military, we have done this for you as much as we have for ourselves."

He looked to White for some kind of indication of his

thoughts, but he was blank, so he went back to the screen.

"A good number of you have volunteered for service, but not nearly enough. I am here to tell you that whatever life you have now; it cannot last without your intervention in this war. A good many of you work in professions that we need to support everything we do, but there are still thousands, probably hundreds of thousands who could serve. Those of us who fight are too few. Some of the officers I know want to begin conscription, but I don't think we need it because I believe those who can, will come forward. Men and women aged between sixteen and sixty, and who are physically fit, come forward. Volunteer to fight beside us, because without you, none of us have a future. What will it be? Keep ducking your duty as a human being, or fight for your future and the future of us all? All those who are able and willing, be sure to notify the captain of whichever vessel you are stationed on, or report to the recruit training camp on Ony. That's all."

The transmission stopped, and Lasure appeared before him once again.

"You said you wanted conscription, but you just asked for more volunteers? You know how many times we have done that since we have been here?"

"I don't want anyone who has been forced into it. I want every man and woman to be a volunteer, and to have a full comprehension of why they are coming forward. If they cannot understand how desperate these times are, then they are no good to us."

"I fail to see how we'll get any more volunteers coming forward than before," replied Lasure.

"I think he might just have done it," added White.

Lasure turned away for a moment as he received a message and slowly looked back to Taylor. His expression had changed entirely, and whatever he had to say was clearly important.

"What is it, Admiral?"

"We've just received intel on a possible location for Erdogan."

Taylor's face suddenly turned to immense concentration.

"Where? Give me everything you have got, right now," he demanded.

"We need to give this some serious thought, Colonel."

"Just give me what you've got!"

Lasure was stunned and a little intimidated.

"This is the number one priority of the human race, Admiral! Send me everything you have, right now. I'll start getting some teams together, and we'll be en route within the hour."

"Colonel, we should…"

"Just get me that information, Admiral!"

With that, he turned and rushed out with Moye at his side, leaving White and Lasure to get on with it. Morris followed on after Taylor but knew better than to stand in his way.

"Colonel, you have no idea what you're getting yourself into."

"A chance to take down Erdogan? I don't care how slim it is. That is all I need to know."

"Colonel, you have been going out there every day, all week. You've not been getting enough rest, and losing personnel and resources quicker than they can be replenished. Your luck only goes so far."

"Just far enough to end Erdogan's life," he replied and continued on at a rapid pace.

Moye reached out and grabbed his arm, attempting to stop him in his tracks, but the power Taylor's Reitech suit had allowed him to brush it off and leave Moye where he stood.

"Colonel Taylor!" he yelled.

Taylor sighed and finally stopped and turned back to the Major.

"What do you want from me, Moye?"

Moye took a deep breath before answering. "I want to see the Colonel Taylor I got to know. I came to trust you because you proved worthy. But you're getting desperate. You're running your people thin and hard, and taking unnecessary risks."

"Unnecessary? Not a single one of my actions has been unnecessary. And I will not stop until I have done what needs to be done."

"Even if it costs the lives of everyone you know. Even

if it costs your own life?"

"Taylor didn't respond for a moment but then shrugged, as if to admit that it was an acceptable situation.

"You've lost yourself, Colonel. Too caught up in revenge to see clearly."

"Yeah, or maybe now I've finally got the focus to get the job done."

He turned and strode onwards. It wasn't long before he stepped into a mess hall where he knew he'd find his people getting some chow.

"Colonel?" Silva asked, spotting Taylor enter.

"Assemble the Regiment. We move out in twenty minutes."

"Silva was speechless for a moment, but he could see Taylor was being serious."

"All right, Inter-Allied, form up!"

There was no enthusiasm from those sat enjoying a brief moment of peace. But Taylor simply turned and left, trusting in the Sergeant Major to get them up and moving. Morris was waiting outside the mess hall as he made his way outside. Jafar was with him.

"You have found Erdogan?" Jafar asked.

"Maybe. Sounds like a good enough lead to give it a shot."

"You would follow any lead," he stated.

Taylor turned and looked at Jafar in surprise.

"Don't you start as well! We're going after this son of

a bitch, and if it fails or we don't find him, we'll pursue the next lead, and the next one after that until we do find him."

"And when we do?"

"We kill him."

"How?" Jafar replied plainly.

Taylor looked surprised. "What do you mean, how?"

"Last time we fought Erdogan…we barely survived."

"Yeah, well that was then, and this is now," he snapped back.

But Jafar appeared unaffected by his outburst.

"What has changed?" he asked Taylor bluntly.

If it had been anyone else, Taylor knew he would not have given the question a second thought or even considered answering, but this was different. He briefly thought for a moment, but he couldn't think of a sensible answer.

"I don't know, maybe my motivation if different. Maybe our situation is more desperate? Maybe…"

He stopped, realising he was grasping at straws.

"I don't have an answer, all right? Okay, Erdogan scares the shit out of me. He's two or three times stronger than Demiran. He outclasses us in every way, and worse, he knows it. He doesn't show the arrogance of those who came before him. I don't know how to kill him, short of sticking a nuke down his throat."

"You know his location, yes? Then nuke it."

"I wish it were that simple."

"Why is it not?"

"Physical confirmation by eye witnesses that Erdogan is dead is all that will suffice. We can never return to Earth for good unless we know he is dead and buried. And this intel we have is probably bullshit, anyway."

"And still we go?"

Taylor nodded. "Yes, because there is still some chance it's him, such a small chance, but one worth risking it for. We drop a nuke and assume he's dead because of it, and he could just lure us into another trap. I want to see his body with my own eyes."

"And if this is a trap?"

"I don't see how."

"Like you didn't see how Kelly and the clones were a trap?" asked Morris who had been lurking behind them.

Taylor was silenced. It almost brought him to tears as he thought about what that had cost him. Finally, he shrugged it off and turned to face Morris.

"Honestly I can't say how I can beat Erdogan, or how any of us can. We've trained harder than ever since we last faced him. Maybe we're up to the task. We'll find a way because we always do. If you can't have faith in that, then we have already lost. I believe we can beat Erdogan, and therefore we will."

It was wishful thinking, but he was starting to believe it. He began to imagine his Assegai plunging into the alien leader's throat, and it brought a small smile to his face. Morris leaned in close.

"You know that next time we see Erdogan, he'll probably kill us all."

"He can try," replied Taylor, "But he's gonna have to be willing to die himself, and I'm not sure he's likely to do that."

"What do you mean?" asked Morris.

"To Erdogan, everything is about him. It's about his rule, his time. But for me, and I hope the rest of you, it's about more than that. I never thought I'd die through all this fighting, but finally I have accepted it if it is necessary. If Erdogan cannot risk the same, then he is finished."

Morris couldn't believe what he was hearing.

"You're not gonna die. You can't."

"Why?"

"Because you've made it this far, why not to the end?"

"My fate was always tied to this war. Maybe I was destined to live just long enough to bring an end to it."

"I don't believe in destiny," added Morris quickly.

"No, and neither did I. But the pieces seem to be falling in to place."

"I think you overthinking this, Colonel."

Taylor could hear the concern in his voice.

"Don't you worry, Captain. I'll be round for as long as you need me."

Twenty minutes later the Regiment was standing before

the transports ready to take them back up to the jump gate enabled vessels in orbit. They all waited for Taylor to say some words of encouragement, and maybe reveal some information on their mission. They looked tired, and yet still keen to go on.

"I know I've been pushing you all hard! That's plain for all to see!" Taylor shouted, "A mission every single day was a lot to ask, and now a second before you've had time to rest. I'd not ask it of you if it weren't absolutely essential! We just received an unconfirmed sighting of Erdogan. Drones in the area have been unable to clarify. Any chance, any fraction of a chance of pinning him down has to be worth a shot. This could be it, or it could be one of many attempts to find that bastard, but I want you to treat everyone like it is the real deal. Because when we finally back Erdogan into a corner, he's gonna come out fighting like something none of you have ever seen before. This is the start of a hunt, are you up for it?"

They cheered in response.

"Load up. Let's move out!"

CHAPTER THREE

It's gonna be him. It's gonna be him. It has to be him, thought Taylor.

He stood over Rains' console aboard a copter and just stared at the display screens, waiting for them to be filled with the Solar System he knew and loved so much.

"You won't make us go any faster," said Rains.

But Taylor was oblivious to his comments before finally turning to him. He knew the Lieutenant had spoken but had no idea what he had said, so he simply started afresh.

"This isn't your bird."

"Come on, Colonel, you think we could have got her repaired that fast? She was beaten up after that last mission."

"Oh, yeah, so she was."

Rains looked concerned that Taylor seemed so out of it.

"There something I should know?"

"Like what?"

"You seem...distracted."

"Never more focused. You'll forgive me if my mind is on just one thing. We take Erdogan down, and we can end this. That's all that is important to me right now."

"And getting us all back alive?"

Taylor shrugged and slowly nodded in agreement, but it was hardly convincing.

"That's reassuring."

"How are you even still alive?"

Rains was silent, despite rarely ever having been in his life.

"How have you made it this far? All the crazy shit you have done, the suicidal missions. You've been shot down more times than I can count. So how are you still alive and untouched by it all?"

"I wouldn't say I'm untouched, but I'm still going, same as you. I could ask you the same questions."

Taylor nodded. "So how have we made it when others die on their first mission along the way?"

"You're not trying to tell me fate is involved?"

Taylor shrugged. "I have no idea, but it would certainly seem we are alive to achieve one last thing before it all ends, or we end it."

"Hey, I want to win this same as you, but I want to live to celebrate the experience, too."

"You always land on your feet, Rains, from no matter how high you fall. I'm sure you'll be fine."

"Coming from you that means almost nothing."

Taylor smiled a little before turning his attention back to the scanners. He saw new information flash up on screen. Rains checked the instruments briefly.

"That's it. We're here."

A moment later the loading bay doors opened, and light flooded into the cockpit.

"Who'd know, travelling light years from one planet to another twice in one day? It's technology even a year ago that we could never have dreamed of. Makes you wonder what other surprises there are in store for us in the future."

"I've had enough surprises for a life time, Eddie."

They saw pulses flash ahead as the ship came under fire.

"Guess they're getting a little tired of us gate crashing their party!" Rains grinned.

He raised the power, and they soared out from the flank of the Diderot. On the scanners Taylor could make out the dozen friendly vessels and a similar number of enemy on their flank. They had jumped almost into orbit, and as the copter surged forward, they were entering Earth's atmosphere in under two minutes. Rains looked at his scanners every two seconds.

"Don't follow us. We don't need that kind of attention right now. Almost made it," he whispered.

Then a blip appeared on the scanner, and Rains brought up a rear display screen to show a single enemy heavy fighter closing on their tail.

"That's not good," he said.

Lights flashed from its pulse cannons opening fire, and Rains took evasive action. Four of the pulses raced past them, but the first skimmed their fuselage, and the copter rocked violently.

"Shit, we can't take many more like that!"

Taylor looked back at the video feed and watched the fighter get them in its sights, but as it was about to fire, a missile trail from the Diderot soared out and struck its engines. It was blown apart, and Eddie let out a sigh of relief, shaking his head in amazement.

"Nice to see somebody has our back."

They got into the Earth's atmosphere and through light cloud cover, half expecting to find a wall of enemy craft awaiting them, but there was nothing. Rains began to level out, and several other craft came up alongside them as they soared up the Adriatic, running in parallel with the coasts of Italy and Croatia.

"Beautiful," said Rains, "Sure wouldn't mind coming back here some day. Some day when I haven't got fighters on my tail and ground interceptors trying to knock me out of the sky."

Taylor said nothing.

"Or maybe it wouldn't be half as much fun."

Still Taylor said nothing. He was watching the terrain pass beneath them.

"So you really think it's him?"

"No idea, Eddie, but it's worth a shot, no matter how small a chance."

"You know all these raids we keep making, or you keep making. All well and good, but what about the vast armies still on Earth?"

"We avoid them. Keep hitting their infrastructure, and keep hunting for Erdogan."

"And if you never find him?"

"Trust me, we'll meet again. Whether I find him or he finds me."

"Sounds like a reckoning."

"It will be."

"Not far out now. We'll be over Padua in two minutes."

"Once we hit the ground, we have a maximum of ten minutes, whether we complete the operation or not. If we haven't called you in sooner, you be at Extraction Point A at the ten-minute marker. Whoever is there at that time, whether it's all of us or none of us, you get going. Reinforcements will be on us like a tonne of bricks after that time. You don't wait around, you hear?"

"Got it!"

"On your feet!" Taylor ordered, heading for one of the side doors.

"We do this and you gotta take some rest, Colonel,"

Silva said, leaning in.

"That an order?"

"We need you at your best, Colonel, and we need to be at our best to get the job done."

"We go where the fight is."

"There'll always be a fight to join. Doesn't mean it always has to be you fighting it, Sir."

Taylor shook his head. He knew it was logical, but it he didn't want to hear it.

They felt the forward thrusters kick in, and they held on tight as they were brought to an abrupt hover.

"Go, go, go!" Rains shouted.

Taylor hit the door release, and once again was out the door in a fearless fashion. Silva shook his head before jumping quickly after him. He hit the ground just beside the Colonel and was surprised to find him standing still but looking cautiously ahead, and then to either side. Silva could see his concern. There was nothing there. They were on the southwest outskirts of the city, and yet there was no sign of life, human or alien. It was as if they'd landed in a ghost town.

"Looks all too familiar," whispered Silva.

"When our people were evacuating, yeah," replied Taylor, "but not anymore. If Erdogan were here, then it would have been with more than a few thousand of his soldiers."

"So they just picked up and left? You think it's a trap?"

"I'd expect to have been hit by now if that were the case. No, I don't see how they could have any inkling of our arrival."

Suddenly, Taylor caught a glimpse of movement out of the corner of his eye and panned quickly to see a single Mech warrior strolling towards them as if taking a walk in the park. It was a bizarre scene that caused Taylor and his platoon to simply stand and stare for a moment as others descended into position behind them.

Finally, the creature raised its rifle. It fired and began falling back to the corner of building it had come from. It got off two shots and disappeared behind the structure. A dozen shots landed where it had been and knocked chunks of concrete from the corner, and yet it had escaped them.

"Move, move, move!" Taylor ordered and rushed forward towards the cover of a low building ahead of them. As he hit it, he edged to the corner and looked around for some sign of the enemy.

"This is no trap. They had no idea we were coming," said Silva as he hit the wall beside Taylor, "Think Erdogan is still here, after all?"

Taylor shook his head. "No idea at all, but I intend to find out."

As he finished speaking, he ran out from cover and made a sprint for the building where the creature had come from. As he got halfway, several pulses struck the ground around him from weapons fired from windows of the buildings up ahead. Silva and several others tried to lay down covering fire and spot for targets, but he couldn't make out much for certain. A few more shots struck the wall and made him duck back for cover.

A pulse skimmed the edge of Taylor's shield. Two more landed close by his feet, but he managed to reach the position where they had first encountered enemy contact. Silva peered around the corner to see Taylor was already looking for targets. He appeared to show no fear at all, but more than that, he seemed to have no regard for his own life. Silva shook his head, knowing there was absolutely nothing he could do about it.

"Oh…what the hell!" He rushed out from cover and sprinted towards Taylor's position.

Pulses struck the ground all around him, but he kept going and hoped for the best. Just as he was about to reach cover, his shield took multiple pulse impacts. It fell from his arm, and the handle broke free, so he let it slide before it hindered his movement. He reached the building beside Taylor and let out a sigh of relief, looking back at his shield. It lay shattered on the ground and smouldered from the heat of the impacts.

"Nice day for a run?" Taylor asked.

"Goddamn it, Colonel, you're going to get us all killed some day."

"We're all gonna die eventually," he said calmly.

Taylor raised his hand and spoke into his comms unit.

"King, come in, you on course this time?"

"Affirmative. Approaching from the north. We have met minimal resistance and are five hundred metres from you."

"Keep moving!" yelled Taylor. "Anders, maintain this position, Matthews take the right flank. Keep going forward!"

Jafar and several others made it to their position and awaited his orders.

"You think Erdogan was here? Or still is?"

Jafar shook his head.

"You're a big help."

"He's right, Colonel," added Silva, "We've not seen a single bit of evidence that he was ever here."

Taylor looked at his watch and sighed.

"We've got a few minutes left. Let's use them."

As he finished, he took the bend where they had seen the first Mech and rushed out without even checking what was around the corner. The others followed suit and found themselves in a street between tall buildings that sheltered them from the firing arc of the Mechs who had been firing on them. They could still hear Anders' platoon exchanging fire with them at their original position.

Up ahead, they could see a small alien transport on the road outside a museum. As they approached, the craft began to lift off. Taylor raised his rifle and began firing, but none of the shots penetrated the thick hull. Several others joined in, but it was quickly gaining altitude quickly and passed out of view over the top of one of the buildings.

"Shit!" Taylor hollered.

His voice was loud and drawn out, to the level that it was clear to all he was irate.

"That can't have been him," said Silva.

"You don't know that!"

"We know the way he travels. You think he'd be travelling in one little ship with no escorts? You know him. He's all about show," replied Silva.

"But we don't know it!"

"It wasn't Erdogan," said Jafar.

They all turned in surprise to look at him and waited for him to go on.

"He was here, but not in that vessel."

"How do you know?" Silva asked.

Jafar pointed to a deep blue shimmer coming from the steps of the museum. It was the kind of cover laid as if for a VIP, and the light was glinting off of it.

"He was here recently."

Taylor looked at his watch.

"All right, sixty seconds, let's find out what the hell he was up to."

Taylor rushed ahead, reaching the stairs to find the cover was so fine in texture it was like silk, though far stronger. He rushed up the steps and through the main door with his rifle held high, expecting to find a target in any moment, but there was nothing. The museum was untouched, with artefacts on show as you'd expect, but without any staff or patrons.

"What on Earth was he doing here?"

"He was studying us," replied Morris.

Taylor hadn't even noticed the Captain was with them until that moment. He shrugged as if asking for Morris to continue.

"I was here before all this kicked off. This museum was untouched by all of the wars and took on thousands of pieces that were rescued from other cities. It's now one of the finest collections in the world and had to be expanded. It's a remarkable museum."

"And yet nobody tried to protect all this?" asked Lang.

"They wouldn't have had time," replied Taylor, "Last war was over before it had really got started. We ran for our lives, took only what we could. So you think he came here as a tourist?"

Morris nodded. "You've told me many times he studies and understands us better than those who came before him. If you had free run of the world, wouldn't you visit a place like this? Lots to learn about the human psyche."

"We almost had him," muttered Taylor, "We came so close. Must have missed him by what, a few minutes?"

"Never had a chance," said Silva, "We acted on this as quickly as we could. This mission was a failure before we ever started."

"But we're getting closer," added Morris, "You think he's studying our culture for any other reason than working out how we're still standing?"

Taylor looked confused.

"I doubt the Krys ever met an enemy who caused them this must trouble. You've killed two of their most powerful and influential figures, and after all they have thrown at us, here we are still fighting."

Taylor turned to Jafar for confirmation.

"I believe the Captain may be right."

"But what more can he learn at a museum?"

"Whatever he hasn't worked out."

An alarm went off on Taylor's watch, and he looked to see they were out of time.

"It's time to move out!"

He got moving, but just a few seconds later he could hear the roar of engines that were not from their own craft. He looked up to see two enemy transports soar into view overhead, and Mechs began to descend towards them.

"Cover!"

The platoon scattered to either side of the street into the cover of the buildings. A few of them began to open fire as Taylor yelled into his mic.

"Rains, we've got trouble. Need an alternate pickup point, and we need it now!"

"If I'd listened to your orders, Colonel, then we'd

already have left your ass behind!"

"Enough of the pleasantries, get us out of here!" Taylor hollered over the sound of gunfire.

Taylor watched as two of the Guardians strode out into the middle of the street and began laying down fire on the vessels hovering overhead. The platoon engaged the Mechs. Taylor looked up; the Guardians were blowing holes in the Mech aircraft, and one of them was already falling out of the sky. But even as several in the platoon were celebrating, they could see dozens of Mechs landing in the street either side of them.

"Rains!" yelled Taylor, "We can't get out of the city like this!"

"What do you want us to do, Colonel?"

He looked around and could see the building the other side of the street was a police HQ. It was eight storeys high.

"We're at the police HQ, thirty metres from the city museum."

"Museum? What the hell are you up to down there?" Rains asked.

"Does the Police HQ have a landing zone on the roof, and if so, can you provide evac from that point?"

As he waited for a response, he shouldered his rifle and took a few shots at one of the Mechs that landed on the street a few metres from where he was sheltering.

"We can do that, but you're gonna have to lay down

some cover fire! ETA two minutes!"

Taylor looked back at the carnage around him. Dozens of Mechs lay dead in the street, and a medic was attended to one of their wounded.

"Up to the roof of the HQ now!" he yelled.

He got to his feet and rushed across the road. The Guardians were still standing in the centre laying down fire without any concern for the enemy gunfire at all. He stopped at the entrance to the HQ and took cover, taking aim at a Mech dropping from the sky and fired a six-shot burst at the creature.

"Come on, move it, Marines!"

The last of them got up to cover the ground, but Fuchs was hit in the hip as he made his way across. He dropped like a stone, but two of the others grabbed him a second after he had fallen down and dragged him onwards and through the doorway. The last of the marines were inside when Taylor shouted to the Guardians.

"Come on!"

They turned and rushed inside. One of them ducked under the doorframe, but the other went right through the frame and smashed it apart with little resistance. The atrium had high enough ceilings for them to stand up straight. There were two elevators ahead and stairs beside them. He rushed to the elevators and hit the buttons to call both down. He turned back to the Guardians as the doors opened.

"Get in!"

They hunched to get inside each of the elevators as he leaned in and pressed the buttons for them before turning back to his own people.

"Go on, move!"

They rushed on up the stairs, and he was quick to follow suit. Eight flights of stairs felt like nothing at all when they knew what being left behind would mean. When Taylor finally reached the rooftop, he found the Guardians blazing away at two enemy craft and driving them away from the rooftop. He took a deep breath and revelled in the air that reminded him where he was. In that moment he knew what he was fighting for. Not just revenge and survival, but the world that was home.

Taylor turned to see Rains' copter and two others. They were flying a few metres above the rooftops, and several Mechs were taking shots at them but not finding their targets. In the distance, they could see the silhouettes of a whole fleet of enemy craft heading their way. Taylor raised his rifle and used the scope to look a little closer, but they were still just dots on the skyline. Even so, he knew that meant they were only a minute or two out, and there were far more than they could handle.

Matthews and Anders rushed onto the rooftop with their platoons as the three copters came in to land. The first hit the ground a little hard, and Taylor ushered the first platoon aboard and then the next. Rains then came in with a perfect landing. He heard the sound of pulse fire nearby and saw two Mechs advancing onto the rooftop from the stairway. The only Guardian still with them returned fire with him, and they were cut down, but several more followed.

"Go!" Taylor ordered those who had stopped embarking.

He kept up the covering fire until all were aboard, and then leapt through the door himself and continued firing as they lifted off the roof. His magazine finally ran dry. He dropped the magazine and pulled out another, but Silva reached forward and closed the door before he could put it into the receiver.

"We're done," said Silva.

Taylor still rammed the magazine home. He felt a hand rest on his shoulder and turned to see Morris.

"We came close," he stated.

"How'd you figure that?"

"Well it wasn't a trap. We got one over on Erdogan. Okay, we got there a little late. But he didn't see it coming and was unable to hide his presence from us. That's got to have rocked him."

"Why?"

"Because he knows we can find him, and because he knows we want to," replied Silva.

"Is this what it has come to?"

The two of them looked confused.

"Hit and run attacks because we don't have the strength to take on his armies? We're fighting a guerrilla war."

"Yes we are," replied Morris.

"And how often in history has that worked out?"

"More than a couple of times."

"Good enough for me," added Silva.

Taylor shook his head in amazement before making his way to the cockpit.

"Cutting it a little fine there, weren't you, Colonel?" Rains asked as he approached.

"Made it out, didn't we?"

Rains pointed at a screen showing the incoming vessels.

"Only just. They got to us, and we'd have been done for."

"Yeah, but they didn't."

"You know, Colonel. If you've got a death wish, I'd rather you fly with someone else."

Taylor's smile disappeared when he looked at the Lieutenant's face and saw that for once he wasn't joking.

"This is your job, Lieutenant. If you don't like it, well that's just tough shit."

Rains guided them up and out into the atmosphere and quickly docked with the Diderot, as they had done so many times before. He didn't say a word until they had come to a standstill, and he knew they were safe. He slowly took off his helmet and turned to Taylor.

"About time somebody said it to you straight, Colonel."

He looked put out by his comments but finally responded. "Well, go on, straighten me out."

"You've been taking liberties with the lives of everyone you know. These are people that love you and would follow you to hell and back. But it's gone further than that now. You're pushing them too hard and taking risks that are beyond fair. We need to kill Erdogan, we all get that, but being reckless with all of our lives isn't the way to do it."

Taylor couldn't believe what he was hearing. His initial reaction was to be defensive, but somehow coming from Rains it made a difference. Rains was a joker and a clown, so for him to question his actions in such a serious manner really drove it home. He opened his mouth to speak but could not find any words. It was starting to sink in, and he felt sick. It reminded him of the moment he saw Eli drop to her knees. He never wanted to feel that way again, and it was a stark reminder of why they were doing all this.

He sat back down in his seat and contemplated everything for the rest of the journey, trying to make sense of it all. He went utterly blank and was oblivious to all around him when Silva gently shook him on the shoulder.

"We're home, or close as," he said.

Taylor looked up. The door was open, and they were back on Ony. He realised he must have been out of it for some time, and it was a sobering experience. He looked up to Rains who had gotten out of his seat and was standing behind Silva.

"You okay, Colonel?" Rains asked quietly.

He gently nodded his head, and Silva helped him to his feet.

"We came close," said Morris.

"Not close enough," he replied.

They stepped out of the copter to find that the sun was going down at their base. He could hear music coming from one of the bars that had been set up nearby.

"Come on, Colonel, time we got you a drink," said Rains.

"Best idea I have heard all day, Eddie."

As they walked away from the copter, he stopped and looked over to Jafar who had remained behind. The alien rarely joined them for their evening entertainment, as he was not usually welcome by many of the troops who gathered for such occasions.

"Come with us," said Taylor.

Jafar did not hesitate to follow them. It was a short walk to the bar, but as they entered, it took just a few seconds to hear a comment about him.

"Fucking alien spy," one muttered.

Taylor turned and squared off against the Army corporal who had said it.

"I didn't see you out there fighting for our freedom today. Apologise."

"I'm sorry, Colonel. I didn't see you there," the man replied before sniggering slightly as his friends joined in.

"No," added Taylor, "Don't apologise to me, to him," he said, pointing to Jafar.

The man looked absolutely stunned for a moment and then burst out laughing.

"Oh, yeah, I'm gonna apologise to one of them," he replied and laughed once again.

The three of his friends found the whole situation hilarious before Taylor reached forward and grabbed him by his uniform. He held him in place and punched him in the face. He was careful this time as to go light, remembering the power of the Reitech suit and the trouble it had gotten him into before.

The Corporal recoiled before the blow, and would have dropped to the ground, were Taylor not holding him up. He clenched his nose as it gushed with blood. His friends leapt up as if to defend him but stopped when Taylor drew his pistol with his free arm and held it up at them.

"Whoa, whoa, whoa!" Silva shouted.

"Stay out of this!" Taylor ordered.

He looked back to the soldiers who had their hands up and showed no signs of a fight.

"His name is Jafar, and you can bet your ass he's done a whole lot more in this war than all of you put together. You don't have the right to question his loyalty. None of us would even have made it this far without his help, so what'll it be?"

The soldier was locked in his grip and still cupping his

bloody nose.

"I'm sorry, I'm sorry, okay!" he yelled.

Taylor finally let go and holstered his pistol.

"Jesus, Colonel, no need to make such a big deal of it."

"No need to make such a trivial deal of what Jafar has done, so don't, and I won't have to."

They carried on to the bar while dozens around them stood silently and stared at the Colonel. As they reached the bar, they found drinks being handed to them before they could even say a word. Music soon started up, and everyone went back to their drinks.

"Walk with me," Taylor said to Jafar.

They headed out of the group and to a quiet spot where Taylor found an ammo crate to sit on and enjoy his drink. Jafar stood waiting for him to speak. He finally grew impatient and spoke first; something he rarely did.

"What can I do for you?" he asked.

Taylor took a deep breath; thinking over what he was going to say, and at last came out with it.

"Our plan is to kill Erdogan, right?"

Jafar nodded.

"What about after he's dead? His armies will be leaderless, but what happens to the Krys?"

"Erdogan took over from Demiran, Karadag, and several other Lords from what I understand. That's more than half of my people. They will support whoever kills Erdogan and shows himself strong enough to take his place."

"I will kill Erdogan, but I cannot lead his people."

Jafar looked confused and waited for him to go on.

"You can. You're the only one who can. You understand both sides. A human will be as distrusted among them as you are amongst my people. You are the only hope."

Jafar looked amazed by the proposition.

"So what do you think?"

"I do not know what it is to lead. I am a soldier, not a leader."

"You and me both. You think I ever wanted any of this? Sure I can lead a few dozen or even a few hundred men. But do you think I ever imagined the responsibly that has fallen on me on all of this? I figure I was just the right guy in the right place to get the job done. And when this is finished, that guy will be you. Do you think they would accept you?"

"If whoever kills Erdogan names me as the head of my people, they will accept it."

"You don't look convinced?"

"I was born and bred to fight, same as the rest of my race. What do I do when I become their leader and there are no more wars to fight?"

"Don't you worry about that, there will always be a war to fight. You don't need to go looking for them. So will you do it?"

"I would not want it, but I will do it if it is what you

wish."

"You aren't my slave, you know? I'd like to think you're my friend. I ask this because not only do I believe you can do it, but we need it."

"Then I shall do it."

"Then let us destroy Erdogan together and see an end to this for good."

CHAPTER FOUR

Taylor woke in his own bed, or as close as to his own as he had. He felt rough for a moment. His body ached and he could barely move, but he sat up, realising he must have slept for a long time. He was remarkably fresh in his head, and only stiff from the many hours he'd been asleep. It was an experience he had long forgotten. For a moment he looked over to see if Eli was there, and then remembered she was gone.

He looked at his watch, and it was the early afternoon. He didn't even remember getting into bed, but he was glad of the rest. He remembered what Rains had said to him. They were damning words, and they had hit hard. He knew he had a duty to be the best he could be, so took some moments for himself. He showered and dressed slowly. When he stepped out of his quarters, Irala was waiting for him.

"So you finally learnt about privacy?"

"I chose to honour your wishes, yes."

"So what can I do for you?"

"You're getting reckless," Irala replied quickly.

"I don't see it that way. I might have pushed it a bit hard the last few days, but now I'm rested and ready to go back out there."

"You want to kill Erdogan. Nobody can understand that better than I."

"So what's the problem?"

"You are valuable to us all, and so is your unit."

"And?"

Suddenly, frenzy came over many in the camp, and Taylor could hear someone calling his name as they made their way towards him through the crowds. It was Silva and he stopped before Taylor.

"What is it?"

"Major Moye, Sir."

"How is he?"

Silva looked stunned and shocked and finally replied.

"He's bad, real bad. Come on, I'll take you to him!"

Taylor rushed on after Silva and was soon at a hospital bed where Moye lay. He was breathing slowly and barely conscious. General White sat beside him in his wheelchair.

Taylor looked to the General who only shook his head. Mitch strode up beside the Major and looked down with a smile. Moye looked into his eyes and smiled in acknowledgment.

"How are you?"

"Not so good," replied Moye, and as he coughed, blood spewed out.

Taylor looked up to see Irala had joined them.

"Can you help him? You have to help him!"

"They already have," White said, "He'd be dead if they hadn't intervened."

"So he's gonna make it, yeah?" Taylor insisted.

He felt a hand on his and looked down to see it was Moye's.

"It's my time, Taylor. But it should have been yours."

Taylor couldn't work out what he meant.

"Ain't none of our time to die," he replied.

Moye shook his head.

"The Mechs that we fought, they were like him," he said, pointing to Jafar. He was standing at the end of the bed. "They were tasked with finding and killing you," he added.

"How do you know this?"

"Because they told me, Taylor. They captured me. My people got me back, but at a great cost."

"They were coming after me? Just me?"

Moye went blank and took a few more breaths before finally passing away.

"Shit… rest easy, my friend," whispered Taylor.

He looked to White.

"That true what he said? That they've got teams hunting me down?"

"We've only got Moye's word, but I'd have no reason to disbelieve him. He was an honest man, and while you hunt Erdogan, why would he not hunt you?"

Taylor had never given it so much as a thought. He'd always had the notion of Erdogan as an almost undefeatable foe who would never need to resort to hunting him down. Then he realised what that meant.

"He fears me? He fears me," he stated.

It was a concept that he'd never contemplated, but it was strangely reassuring.

"He knows you're onto him, he has to," added White, "The fact you were close on his tail on that last mission cannot have gone unnoticed. That'll put him on guard, but it has also rattled him."

"Yeah, he's rattled. He can see there's a chance he can lose this now. For all the armies he has in the universe, he can't threaten us here, and he can't protect his assets from our lightning attacks."

"I guess he tried the obvious choice, attacking us here. Now he's trying the next one, kill you. He knows how valuable you are to our cause."

"But this would go on without me," replied Taylor.

"None of us could have come this far without you, Colonel. Something tells me that you have a vital part to play in ending all of this."

"I won't hide from him."

The General shook his head.

"None of us would ever ask it of you. You are vital because of the work you do and what that means to everyone around you. We take you off the frontline and keep you safe, and all of that is lost. We have to keep risking your life to maintain what hope we have."

Taylor looked at the body of Moye and then to White.

"I want information on where the Major encountered this enemy force. Where, when, every detail you can get me."

"You're going after them?"

"If they're hunting me down, they'll find me eventually, General. I'd prefer that happened at a time and place of my choosing."

"We'll have to run this by Admiral Lasure."

"You can run it by him, but that's what I'm doing."

"You know you have a serious problem with authority, Colonel?"

"Yes, Sir, but just as you say, I was made this way for a reason, ain't no way I'm changing."

'Then you'd better speak to the Admiral yourself. You may have placed him there, but he has proven himself up to the task."

With that, he turned and left with Silva and Jafar at his side. When he got outside the hospital, he found Morris and King waiting for him.

"Is it true?" King asked, "Is there some kind of special unit chasing you?"

"Chasing us," replied Taylor, "They know what a bunch of ultimate badasses we are and figure they can't take much more of it."

They all laughed for a moment, but it was cut short as King continued.

"Seriously, Mitch, they are coming for you, aren't they?"

Taylor nodded. "Bet your ass they are. And we're going to find them before they find us."

"What did you have in mind?"

"Form up the Regiment. We move out at 1500 hours. We're going hunting."

Taylor left them and headed for the HQ. Only Jafar continued on with him, but as they got halfway, Irala appeared beside them.

"You know how irritating that gets? Just appearing out of the blue?" Taylor asked and continued onwards.

"You told me," Irala replied bluntly.

"Well you didn't seem to get the message."

Irala appeared to completely ignore the topic.

"You intend to go after this new enemy, this force that was established to hunt down and kill you?"

"Will nobody let this go?" Taylor asked.

"We cannot agree with this course of action, and neither will we support it. We will recommend your Admiral denies your request to do so."

"Good luck with that," said Morris.

Irala looked back at him in surprise.

"Good luck telling the Colonel what he can and can't do. Say what you want, we're going after those bastards."

Taylor carried on regardless and went straight to the secure comms room of the HQ and patched in a call to the Diderot, only to find it answered immediately by Lasure, as if he had been awaiting the call.

"Colonel Taylor, I know why you're calling."

Taylor nodded.

'Then you know what I need. One sizeable vessel and a couple in support, will you provide them?"

Lasure shook his head.

"You know I have all the respect in the world for you, Colonel, but I cannot support this. I will not pave the way for you to go to your own death."

"Have you that little faith in me?" Taylor asked in amazement, "Do you not remember how you got to be Admiral? I had faith in you, Sir, and I made sure the right thing was done when it needed to be. I don't ask for much right now. Only that you trust in me."

Lasure thought about it for a few moments. It was an uncomfortable silence, but Taylor knew he could not refuse him.

"I'll do this, Colonel, but only because I owe you. I do not support this action and do not believe it is in the best interests of this fleet. I will give you one frigate, the

Baron, and two light destroyers, The Margot and Intruder. They're good ships with good captains. Far from the best we've got, but they'll serve you well."

"Thank you, Admiral, and don't worry. I've survived a lot worse. Erdogan thinks he can take me out, and I intend to prove him wrong. I get this done, and then we finish him for good."

"I've heard that too many times, Taylor. I'll believe it when I see his lifeless body with my own eyes, but go, and good luck, my friend. Lasure out."

The transmission ended, and Taylor strolled out of the building with a smile on his face.

"I can't believe anyone could be so happy about heading out to face their hunters," said Morris.

'They killed Moye, and they intend to kill us all. It's time for a little payback."

He turned to Silva.

"You know the deal. Have everyone formed up at landing zone G for 1430."

"Yes, Sir."

Time passed quickly, and Taylor soon found himself formed up in front of his unit before an operation, as he had been so many times before. And just as always, they waited for his words of inspiration. But this time he felt no enthusiasm for the task at hand, only an iron will to overcome it to get to Erdogan himself.

"I'm sure many of you have heard what we're doing

here! Somewhere out there is an elite fighting force that has been tasked with hunting me down and killing me. Me! The enemy sees me as that much of a threat. What they don't see is that I am just the driving force of you lot. Every one of you is as capable a fighter as I am. They think this is an easy task. I want to prove them otherwise!"

They cheered in support of his words.

"I don't know what to expect with this enemy force, but they are superior fighters than most of what we have faced before. Have your wits about you at all times, and be ready for anything! Load up!"

Taylor was last aboard and made his way through to Rains' cockpit as he always did.

"The Admiral snubbing you this time?" Rains asked.

"How do you mean?"

"We usually travel in style, not aboard that old hulk."

"The Baron? What's wrong with her?"

"She's fifty years old, Colonel. She's a relic of a bygone era."

"Aren't we all?"

Rains shrugged.

"She got jump capacity?"

Rains nodded.

"She was one of the first upgraded as a favour to her Captain, apparently."

"Well then, what's the problem?"

Rains went silent as they lifted off of the surface and

headed for their expeditionary fleet. He soon caught sight of the Baron and could see what Rains was complaining about. It was an antiquated hulk. Broad and flat nosed. Its boxy shape was in stark contrast to the upgraded engines that had been supplied by the Aranui.

"Looks like she's packing some serious armour."

"Oh, yeah, sure, she might as well be an upscaled Mastiff. All armour, no manoeuvrability."

"Sounds like my kind of style," joked Taylor.

Rains saw he couldn't shake Taylor, so he gave up. It wasn't long before they came in to land on the Baron, and yet Rains was still shaking his head as their landing gear touched down. Taylor stepped aboard to find the Captain awaiting him and giving a formal greeting to come aboard. Taylor saluted as he stepped down the ramp and then reached out to shake the Captain's hand casually. He'd never met him before, but he was in his fifties at least, and two parallel deep scars ran down his face from his forehead and across both cheeks. He was a burley looking man, standing a few centimetres taller than Taylor and rivalled his broad shoulders even when Taylor was in armour.

"Welcome aboard the Baron, Colonel. It is an honour to have you and your unit aboard. I am Captain Barclay at your service."

He spoke with a deep throaty voice, but also a well educated one. It was clear he had gotten the finest schooling in Britain and sounded like an older, gruffer version of Jones. He turned his attention to Jafar who made his way to Taylor's side. Taylor was expecting trouble and opened his mouth to speak, but Barclay got out ahead of him.

"So this is your alien ally we have heard so much about? Sergeant?"

The Captain strolled over and offered his hand in a surprising gesture. Jafar looked to Taylor as if unsure how to react. Taylor simply nodded for him to continue. He took Barclay's hand and shook with a firm shake. "Jafar," he added.

"I've heard a lot about you, Sergeant. Can't say I ever imagined I would call one of you an ally, but you've more than proven yourself to us all. It is an honour to have you aboard."

Jafar was as shocked, as was Taylor.

"I presume you will be eager to set off?" Barclay asked.

"You have the reports from the attack on the French cruiser the Tourville?"

Barclay nodded.

"A good friend of mine was aboard that vessel, and he died protecting her. Major Moye. But from what he told us before he died, that attack was meant for me. He said there was an elite task force sent after me. They breached the vessel and killed a number of personnel before bugging out."

"They retreated?" asked Barclay in amazement.

"You're just as surprised as I was to hear the news. Have you received the action reports and location information?"

"We have."

"Then take us to the location of the battle. It's time the hunters became the hunted."

"Very well, Colonel. Will you accompany me to the bridge?"

Taylor followed on as the Captain led the way.

"What is your plan for hunting this enemy task force?"

"They want to find and kill me, so I'm going to give them a chance."

"You're going to use yourself as bait?"

"Yes, why not? They'll surely find me eventually. That's a great heap of shit I don't need hanging over me."

"Eloquently put, Colonel, but I get the idea. How do you intend on announcing your presence?"

"I've got a few ideas."

"Coordinates are plotted. We're ready to jump on your orders, Colonel."

"In your own time, Captain."

Taylor watched the bridge crew as they went about their procedures, turning his attention to the four metre-wide display of the space for a last few moments before they left. There were dozens of Navy vessels stationed in orbit of Ony, and he could see that production of a defence grid barge was well underway. The jump gateway then opened before them and obscured their view. The two escort destroyers passed through the gateway first, and they soon followed suit.

"I've never got used to it. This kind of travel," stated Taylor.

"It certainly makes life easy," replied Barclay.

"Yes, and immensely unpredictable. How can you plan for defence when the enemy can be on you with no warning at all?"

"Then be thankful that they have such limited access to the technology."

Taylor agreed. "Yes, for if they ever manage to reverse engineer it, we're in more trouble than you can imagine."

The three ships passed safely through the gateway the other side, and it closed up behind them. Within seconds, they were struck by light debris they could see floating about space before them.

"Looks like they had a hell of a fight."

They could see the debris of one of the smaller support vessels and a number of fighters, as well as debris that Taylor could only imagine came from the Tourville.

"They had a rough time of it," said Barclay.

"Yeah, and I don't see any sign of damage to enemy craft."

"They must have hit them hard and fast."

Taylor tried to imagine what could have done it, and Barclay was quick to pose the question.

"What did this? A large vessel would have torn them

apart, but how could lesser craft get the drop on them? I'd expect a few enemy losses at least. The Tourville is a powerful vessel with a fine crew."

Taylor nodded in agreement.

"Send out teams to investigate the wrecks. Let's try and get an idea of what went on here."

"It's all in the file," replied the Captain.

"No, the crew of the Tourville who survived have no idea how it went down. When they were struck, it happened hard and fast. The bridge crew were taken out and all recording equipment destroyed. All we know at this stage is that the Tourville was boarded with little resistance. Let's avoid that happening a second time around."

Barclay started sending out his orders to have the crews prepared.

"So what now?" he then asked Taylor.

"We sit and wait. Learn what we can."

"You expect they'll come back this way?"

"I would. Investigative teams would be easy pickings, and they must know there's a chance I would have come along to see it for myself."

"So what is stopping us from suffering the same fate?"

"The fact we know they're coming. I need to know everything we can about this attack. Next time they come for us, I want to know exactly how they're gonna do it. Let's shoot these bastards down before they have another chance at this kind of devastation. Almost two hundred crew lost their lives aboard the Tourville, and countless more from her support vessels."

"Sounds like we could have done with a little more support."

"Damn right, Captain. I need somewhere to go over the last recordings of these vessels, if you can salvage them."

"I'll have them with you within the hour. You may use my quarters while you are aboard."

"Thank you, please have Captain Morris and Sergeant Jafar sent up to me."

The Captain acknowledged and showed him to his quarters before leaving him in peace. The Captain's quarters were spartan to say the least. The only decoration in the room was a single picture of his family secured to the wall beside his desk. The room looked like it saw little use, and Taylor liked that about the Captain. He could already see he was a man loved by his crew, and that was a valuable asset.

Taylor, Morris, and Jafar had been going over the few reports they had received from the Tourville when Barclay entered.

"We've recovered the last recorded data from the Lampo. A small destroyer, it was the hulk we saw when we first arrived. We also managed to salvage a little data from one of the fighters. It's not much, but it's all we can get."

"Thank you, Captain. Please join us so we have a fresh pair of eyes on all of this."

Taylor brought up the new information and projected it onto the table. He took them to the point in time thirty minutes before the attack. They had the ship's technical logs but no video information at all. He went through the info minute by minute until he reached the point three minutes before the attack began.

"What is that?"

"Power fluctuation. Primary power loss for a brief period and secondary power kicked in to take up the slack," said Barclay.

"What would cause it?"

"All kinds of things. Work being done by engineers, a failing electrical component."

Taylor brought up the log from the fighter and matched up the time codes until he stopped and pointed at a similar power fluctuation.

"What are the chances of that? Happened at the exact same moment, to the second. What are the chances, Captain?"

Barclay looked confused as he studied the two.

"The odds of it happening are incredibly slim, unless the cause was the same for both."

"What would be the effect?"

"Not a lot, a brief power fluctuation. Lighting and life support can be interrupted for a second or two."

Taylor shook his head as he tried to figure it out.

"Weapons systems?"

"Nothing that would be noticeable."

Taylor looked back over the data from the Lampo.

"What's this?" he asked Barclay.

"Proximity scanner sensors. Looks like they failed during the power flocculation."

"Moye seemed to think the Mechs just came out of nowhere. One minute they were fine, and next they had Mechs swarming through their vessel. No one could work out how they made it in without being spotted."

"The cloaking technology we used to see with Karadag, they could have used it to get nearby with smaller craft. Maybe get in undetected?"

Taylor looked to Barclay for answers. His face suddenly turned white as it all fitted together in his head.

"If the proximity scanners were damaged or tampered with, then boarding craft that were invisible by sight or scan would be able to breach the hull without warning. You'd never even know where they'd latched on unless you could get visual confirmation. They could hit anytime."

Taylor quickly lifted his comms unit.

"This is Colonel Taylor. Calling all hands to arms. Prepare to be boarded!"

Barclay looked at him in horror.

"You don't think?"

"Yes I do. This was the perfect bait to get us right where they wanted us. They were never hitting us with force, but with stealth. Spool up the gateway, and get us the hell out of here!"

Barclay tapped the comms channel on the desk beside him, but just as he opened his mouth to speak, he was silenced as the lights flickered, and they felt the power surge before coming back online.

"It's begun," said Silva.

"Get us back to Ony; best thing we can do right now is get out of here. At least back there we can get some help."

"This is the Captain. Plot a course to Onekaka now!"

They rushed out of the Captain's quarters to find the crew looked stunned by what they were hearing. Finally, his flight officer turned and stuttered as she responded.

"Gateway won't activate, Sir."

Oh, shit! What have I got us into? Taylor thought.

"Get me engineering!" Barclay bellowed.

Taylor raised his comms channel.

"Prepare to repel borders. We've got hull breaches incoming. Location unknown. 1st Platoon to the bridge and secure it, 2nd Platoon to engineering and hold there, 3rd Platoon, you're on patrol."

"This can't be happening," Barclay whispered to himself.

"I guess you wanted to bait the enemy. Well, you've done it now, Colonel," said Silva.

A few seconds later, a call came through to the bridge that opened with small arms fire.

"We've got enemy contact at Level Four on the

starboard side. We can't hold them...we..."

Several more shots rang out, and the transmission ended. Taylor turned to see a few members of 1st Platoon had arrived.

"Hold this position. Do not let them get through you, got it?"

He turned back to Barclay.

"You want to get us out of this? Get the engines going. The only way the Tourville made it home was because she jumped out. Left here much longer and she'd have been torn apart. Get us up and running!"

He turned to leave, but Barclay called out.

"Colonel? Where are you going?"

"To try and thin them out. You've got your job to do, and I've got mine. Get us moving, Captain!"

He rushed to the door.

"1st Platoon, you hold here unless I tell you otherwise. Jafar, Silva, on me."

He rushed onwards with just the two of them at his side.

"Running a little thin, don't you think?"

"It'll have to do, Silva," replied Taylor.

They all had their rifles on them, but no one had shields.

"This is a monumental fuckup of a defence," stated Silva.

"We underestimated our attackers, that's for sure."

He knew it was the greatest underestimation he'd heard

in a long time, to the extent that it even brought a smile to Silva's face.

"Where are we heading?" he asked.

"Sweep and clear, and if we can get to either the armoury or our copter to pickup shields, all the better."

"Copter is closer."

Taylor nodded and went ahead to lead the way. He took a bend and could hear movement, so he ducked back behind a support beam, holding his rifle up at the ready. The steps were lightweight, so he assumed they were human, but he wanted to be sure. Three crewmembers took the bend and stopped in horror at the sight of him. They were carrying Reitech carbines that they had drawn from the armoury, but without the exo-suits even the carbines were hefty loads to lug around.

"Colonel, what's going on?"

"We're heading for the hangar bay. Fall in and form a rear guard."

He went quickly past them, and they tagged on. Gunfire echoed out ahead, and Taylor took a corner to see the flank of one of the enemy firing its weapon. It was using some kind of forearm-mounted pulse weapon and carried a shield in its other. The Mech's armour was sleek and compact, much like what Jafar used to wear. It was also jet black and made them appear as a shadow. He felt a tingle run down his spine, and he now understood why they were so terrifying.

Without any more hesitation, he lifted his rifle and took a well-aimed burst at the creature's head. The first shot glanced off its helmet, but the second and third penetrated, and it dropped down dead before it could turn to face him.

"Not so bad," he muttered to himself.

Even before he had finished, another one of them took the corner with its shield held before it. Taylor fired a few shots, but nothing could get through.

"Grenades?" Silva asked as he ducked back for cover.

"This close to firing up a gateway? Hell, no."

"We need to live long enough to get that far," he added.

"We can't face them like this. We need to get to our gear."

He pointed off to another room next to them and a door they could see on the far side.

"That way! Move!"

He leaned out and fired a few shots for covering fire before following the others. Silva led the way through another few rooms and corridors until they reached the entrance to the hangar. Silva leaned in just enough to see two of the creatures pacing across the deck. He caught another glimmer of movement and could see it was Rains sitting just inside a side door of one of the copters. Two other crewmembers lay dead not far from the craft. Rains looked terrified. Silva looked to the nose of the copter he was in and could see the Reitech chain gun had a magazine loaded; he could only hope it had ammunition. Silva gestured towards the gun and signalled for him to put down fire before turning back to the group.

"Rains is gonna put down some fire from that nose gun, then we hit them, okay?" he said to the group, as Taylor peered around for a look with his own eyes.

"He starts that gun firing, and they're gonna hit back hard. No hesitation, you hear?"

Silva nodded in approval, but the sailors with them looked terrified and barely able to move. Taylor couldn't blame them. He remembered the first time he saw the Mechs, and these were a far more terrifying enemy than they were accustomed to. Taylor watched Rains climb carefully into the cockpit, but he stumbled as he dropped into the seat, and the creatures heard him. They turned to fire, but Taylor took it as his chance. He raised his rifle and fired a six-shot burst into the back of one of them. It dropped face first to the deck. The other turned on him quickly, and pulses smashed the frame beside him as he ducked back for cover.

A moment later, they heard the nose gun on the copter spool up, and then a split second later the almost deafening sound of the weapon. It began firing at such a rate you could not differentiate one shot from another. Taylor peered around the corner. The shots of the Gatling gun smashed into the creature's shield and forced it back. Finally, the shield was torn apart, and it took the full brunt of the weapon. The Gatling gun tore a half metre hole in its chest, almost severing its body in two, and it crumpled dead to the deck.

Rains took his finger off the trigger and sat back with a sigh of relief before making his way back to the side door. Taylor approached the pilot, but as he got halfway, he felt a hand grab hold of his ankle. He looked down. The first creature he shot had locked him in a vice grip, and only his exo skeleton stopped his bones from breaking. The alien raised its other arm to fire at him, but Taylor smashed it away with his rifle and then stomped on its face five times until the helmet gave way and collapsed. He took aim at the seemingly lifeless body and fired three shots into the head to be certain.

"Damn they don't die easy."

Then they heard the intercom activate.

"This is the Captain speaking. Prepare to jump in five... four...three...two..."

Taylor half expected the jump to fail but was amazed on hearing the Captain say jump. He felt the bizarre gravity shift they always did as they passed through. Rains let out another sigh of relief.

"We're not out of the shit yet," said Taylor.

CHAPTER FIVE

"We're through!" yelled the flight lieutenant.

Barclay activated an open channel immediately and put out his emergency message.

"This is Captain Barclay of The Baron. We have enemy combatants aboard and request immediate support."

A few moments later the Admiral's voice came over the line.

"This is Lasure. What the hell is going on over there, Captain?"

"Sir, we have an unknown number of enemy combatants aboard this vessel. We need additional support from Marine detachments immediately!"

The line went silent for a moment until finally Lasure responded.

"Maintain your position. We will despatch assistance to you."

"They better be quick," muttered Barclay as the transmission ended.

As he said it, they heard gunfire ring out from just outside the bridge, and the squad of marines quickly returned fire.

"I need some eyes on what's going on. Get me something!" Barclay ordered.

"Sir, video feeds are down. All we've got is audio comms, and I'm having trouble reaching a lot of the crew."

* * *

"We're taking heavier fire in engineering!" shouted Lang over the comms.

Taylor was passing a shield out to Silva and grabbing his own when he heard the message.

He froze for a moment and said thoughtfully, "Why would they still be going for the engines when we're already back at Ony?"

"They don't want to stop us. They want to destroy us," said Silva.

"If they reached the Aranui reactor and hit it with enough explosives, what would that do?"

"Nothing good," replied Silva.

"It would likely destroy the ship," added Jafar bluntly.

"We have to get moving, now!"

As he said it, Jafar opened one of the storage lockers on

the side of the copter and pulled out one of the 50CMG 'pigs'.

"Can you handle that?" Taylor asked him.

The pig was as long as Jafar was tall, and they could see he was straining slightly to carry it, but it would have to do. They rushed on towards engineering and could hear the echo of gunfire from various locations as they did so. They found two bodies of their own platoon and several more crewmembers lying dead nearby. There was no time to check if any were still alive.

A crossroads lay ahead, and as they reached it, one of the creatures stepped out before them. Taylor squeezed the trigger of his rifle almost immediately. The Mech took the first of his shots on its shield before advancing and barging him into the sidewall. Silva tried to take aim, but as he did so, Taylor drove his knee up into the creature and forced it back so that it could not bring its weapon to bear. The alien warrior's forearm-mounted pulse cannon came around his shield, and he grabbed it in time as it opened fire. Pulses ripped into the corridor beside him.

He smashed down onto the weapon with his shield until it stopped firing, but the creature countered with a swift kick to his abdomen, smashing him back against the sidewall. But it opened up the creature to Jafar's line of sight. He pulled the trigger on the pig, and the high calibre rounds resonated through the corridor as five shots tore holes in the Mech. It collapsed at Taylor's feet. He was still clinging to the wall where he had been thrown, and blue blood had coated the front plate of his armour where the massive rounds had punched holes through his attacker.

"Little close, don't you think?" he asked Jafar.

"What are you complaining about? You're still alive," Silva asked.

"Those things are fast, too fast."

"From a world not far from mine. Good warriors. A small elite," said Jafar.

"Good, I don't wanna have to face many more like that. Let's keep moving."

He looked back to the crewmembers that had stayed back behind Jafar and Silva. They still looked terrified.

"How far to engineering?" he asked them.

"Just..just...not far now," one of them stuttered.

"All right, just stick with us and cover our asses, you hear?"

He turned and carried on. The sounds of gunfire up ahead soon grew louder. He knew they were heading for the right place and didn't have time to be cautious, and true enough they soon had the enemy in sight. They could see three of their own battling one of the creatures in hand-to-hand combat. Several others were dug in at the entrance to the engineering wing. Boxes were piled high with spare shields like a small fort.

Taylor immediately took out a grenade and went to activate it.

"This close to the reactor?"

"We don't clear this lot, then we're all dead anyway, Sergeant."

He activated the grenade and tossed it past the group that were fighting, and into the corridor the enemy were firing from. An explosion rang out that silenced everyone. It gave one of the marines an opening to thrust his Assegai into the one they had been struggling to take down. The room went silent for a moment as dust and debris began to settle.

The silence was broken by a shriek as if some kind of battle cry, and a group of the Mechs stormed out from the breach and rushed towards them. Taylor opened fire, as Jafar swung around the huge 50BMG and held down the trigger so that his shots strafed the charging group. His shots were the only ones to penetrate the shields. One of the rounds blew a hole right through a shield but missed the creature behind it; another put two shots right through, hitting the Mech dead centre. The shield had taken the velocity out of the blow and didn't go through the body armour.

Taylor armed another grenade and tossed it over the top of the charging horde in case any followed after them. As he had recovered, one of the Mechs descended onto him, and he held out his shield to protect himself, turning slightly to take the impact. The beast brushed off his shield and ran straight into one of the crewmembers behind him. The sheer weight of the beast crushed the man as it continued on to try and finish off the other two. Taylor raised his rifle and fired a burst into its back. The shots hurt the creature but didn't kill it. It snapped around and rushed at him. A blade extended out of its arm alongside its pulse cannon, and it thrust for him. He raised his shield, but the blade pierced through cleanly like an Assegai. It only missed his left arm by a few centimetres, and the tip had stopped in front of his face.

"Shit!" he yelled in shock. He raised his shield and pushed his rifle through under and fired a few rounds, but they couldn't penetrate the frontal armour of the Mech, and it pulled its blade free of his shield and thrust once again. He knew not to take any thrust now so tilted his shield and deflected the blow.

"Down!"

It was Jafar.

He ducked, and Jafar swung the hulking 50BMG and hit the Mech with it like a club. The Mech folded from the force of it as if being hit by a truck, but Jafar did not let up as it crumpled to the ground. He took hold of the gun barrel and raised it up, smashing it down like a pile driver into the creature's head. The force of the impact smashed its helmet and fractured its skull.

Taylor turned around and saw Silva get hit by a pulse in the inner side of his arm. He cried out in pain and dropped his Assegai. Jafar lifted up the pig and held down the trigger until Silva's attacker was riddled with shots and fell. Taylor rushed at the last one with his shield held before him. The creature turned to engage, but he spun around it, smashing the lower edge of his shield into the back of its leg so that it dropped onto one knee. Before it could recover, he plunged his Assegai down into its collar and ran it down to the hilt.

He pulled out the blade, and it spewed more blue blood out across him as he looked at the carnage surrounding them. As many of their own lay dead as those of the enemy. He rushed to Silva's side.

"How is it?"

"Not so bad," he replied with a groan.

Taylor looked closer to see the shot had clipped the upper inside of his arm and gone right through.

"Gonna hurt like a son of a bitch, but you'll be okay."

"Great," he replied sarcastically.

"Colonel Taylor?" Barclay asked over the comms.

"Taylor here," he replied casually.

"Colonel, I have two US Marine transports requesting permission to come aboard."

"Well for goodness sake let them land."

No response came back.

"Can you walk?" Mitch asked Silva.

"I'm wounded, not crippled," he replied defensively.

Taylor reached down and helped him to his feet.

"Squad stays put. I'll take what I came with and head for

the docking bays and try and organise this bloody mess."

Silva gathered up his rifle and winced, but he managed the weight despite the wound. Jafar still lugged the cumbersome pig, now coated in blood at the receiver end where it had caved in the skull of a Mech warrior. Taylor felt the familiar aches and pains that always came with a close quarters battle with the enemy. Far from letting it get him down, it was just a reminder that he was in the right place.

Taylor led them back the way they had come and walked over the same dead bodies they had the first time. The corridors were quiet now, too quiet. Taylor didn't know whether to mourn the dead or be concerned of whatever was left for them to deal with.

"Don't move!" a voice yelled.

Taylor recoiled back and raised his rifle.

"Identify yourself!" he shouted in return.

"Sergeant Whitaker, US Marine Corps!"

"Colonel Taylor…"

He couldn't think of anything to tag on, but felt it was all the introduction he would need. He lowered his rifle, stepped out slowly, and found himself in front of four marines. Their uniforms were perfectly cleaned and pressed beneath their armour. The Sergeant looked close to thirty and like he'd seen his fair share of combat, but the others couldn't have been old enough to have served in the wars until very recently.

"Sorry, Colonel, we couldn't get a good eye on you before," said Whitaker.

He reached the Sergeant and then saw there were at least another two-dozen marines behind him.

"Let us take over from here, Colonel," said Whitaker.

"You in charge of these boys?" Taylor asked. He looked them over and laughed as he saw that almost half were women, "and girls," he added.

"Yes, Sir."

They all carried the same Reitech equipment he was intimately familiar with. They moved with purpose and experience.

"Let us sweep and clear, Colonel. You can stay put and protect the landing bay," insisted Whitaker.

He watched Silva slump down onto an ammo box, and the two remaining crewmembers followed suit.

"Please, Colonel, let us do our job."

Taylor hated being laid up. He found it difficult to relinquish responsibility to somebody else, but he could see they needed it.

"Your people ever faced Mech warriors?"

"Yes, Sir," he replied quickly.

Taylor was surprised, but he knew he shouldn't be.

"They aren't like what you have faced before. Nothing like. Faster, stronger, better armoured; their suits are smaller and yet more resilient to our weapons. They are an elite that you would never wish to face."

"We can handle it, Colonel," replied Whitaker confidently.

"I hope so. We'll hold here, but I'm having the Captain put this ship down on Ony ASAP."

"Are you sure that is wise, Colonel?"

"What is aboard is dangerous, but they are few, and we are many. A situation we have rarely known in this war."

"We've got this, Colonel."

"Good luck to you."

The fresh Marine platoon rushed on into the depths of ship. Taylor hoped they were prepared for what was to come, but he knew how exceptional the circumstances were. He lifted his comms unit.

"Captain Barclay."

"Speaking," he finally replied.

"Take us in and put us down ASAP."

"Why?" he asked in amazement.

"Because we still don't know exactly what we're dealing with. Down there we have help and manpower in abundance. I don't want to die alone up here, Captain."

"I will have to request permission to land. I doubt we'll get it," he replied.

"Then don't ask. You might be in command of this ship, Captain, but I am in command of this mission, and I say put this ship down on Ony. Anyone has a problem with that, and they can take it up with me."

"Aye, aye, Sir."

Taylor looked at Jafar. He had set up his pig on one of the tripods overlooking the main and one of the secondary entrances to the docking bay. Silva had taken a seat on a box nearby and Rains' legs dangled from the side of the copter he sat in, a rifle resting across his legs.

"Guess this didn't all go to plan?" asked the Lieutenant.

Taylor shook his head as he thought over everything that had happened.

"Every time I think I have Erdogan figured out, he springs something new on us. I thought he'd want to try and finish me himself. I thought his ego would allow for nothing else."

"He's scared," added Silva.

Taylor looked unsure; it wasn't a position he had considered.

"You really think so?"

"You've rocked him. He's getting hit in lightning attacks that he cannot stop. For all he knows, we could turn up on his doorstep or at his bedside and slit his throat. You've gotten too close."

"Not close enough," he sighed.

"Hey, Taylor?" Rains asked casually, "Tell me something."

He nodded for Eddie to go on.

"Are you the hunter or the hunted? Seems like...well...I don't know anymore."

Taylor had no answer for it. None of them spoke

another word until they felt the ship put down on the surface of Ony. The docking bay ramps opened, and they found more than a hundred soldiers and marines surrounded them. Guardians filled their ranks also. In between them was a large-scale body scanner to detect for clones.

"What is this?" Rains asked.

"It's all right," Taylor said quietly, "They're right to be suspicious. I'd do just the same."

Barclay strode out into the docking back to Taylor.

"We've been ordered to clear the ship while the Marine detachment scours the decks."

Taylor nodded and headed out down the ramp of the docking bay beside the Captain. As he reached the clone scanner, he turned back to see they had less than a hundred personnel with them.

"This all that made it?"

"So far."

Taylor knew the frigate would have had a crew close to two hundred, as well as those he had taken aboard.

"I'm sorry," he said softly to Barclay.

But Barclay stood firm and upright and quickly contested his statement.

"You will not apologise to me, Colonel. The losses we suffered are tragic, and they will not be forgotten, but it was not you would caused their deaths."

"But I led you out there. It was my mission and my

plan."

"And you got us out alive. I will gladly serve alongside you again, Colonel."

Taylor couldn't believe Barclay could be so understanding. He had the same stiff upper lip and willpower that Jones had always held, and it was admirable.

"Lay down your weapons!" one of the officers awaiting them ordered.

Jafar had carried the 50CMG out with him and looked to Taylor for confirmation. He nodded in approval before unclipping his rifle and handing it to an armourer and his assistants who awaited them nearby. His pistol and Assegai were next, as well as the two grenades on his webbing and all of his ammunition. He was then ushered forward to the scanner. It was larger than any other he had seen before, broad enough for ten men to walk through and tall enough to accommodate even a Guardian.

As he neared the device, he began to wonder if the clone of Jones knew what he was before he turned on them. He began thinking if any of them would know if they truly were who they thought they were. He was first through the scanner with Barclay. They passed through without incident and turned to watch the others follow after them. To Taylor's relief, they all passed the test.

"Please come with me, Colonel," said a Captain.

He did not recognise the woman who stood almost as tall as he was and spoke with a thick French accent. Taylor didn't question the request, but he knew he was in for trouble. The mission had been the biggest disaster since the debacle with the clones he brought back under the guise of Kelly and his people. Taylor had no excuses and felt more angry with himself than anyone else could.

Jafar followed him and Barclay had come, too.

"I'll be sure to make sure you do not suffer because of this. This is on me," Taylor said to him.

"Nobody can fault you for it, Colonel. My biggest concern right now is laying our dead to rest, caring for the few wounded, and to find replacements."

"Good luck finding them. Personnel are the one resource we don't have in abundance."

"Tourville was pretty screwed after that last mission. I'd suggest you put in a request with the Admiral for her crew to join you until such time as they can return to their ship. Should give you a chance to train up new personnel."

"Think he'd go for it?"

"The Admiral will go with whatever gets us the most ships in operation. They may not like it, but these times call for exceptional measures."

"Half the crew French aboard a British warship? It's a novel idea."

Taylor couldn't believe how calm and jovial the Captain could be at such a time, but he remembered Jones was just the same. He suffered deep down the same as the rest of them, but his confidence inspired like nothing else could.

He was led through into HQ and ushered into the comms centre where he found the Admiral. General White stood next to him balanced on one crutch. He was about to speak but was surprised to see Irala standing opposite them.

"One big happy family now, are we?" he asked.

"In a manner of speaking," said White.

Taylor could tell from the General's tone that something wasn't quite right, but he couldn't understand what it could be, so put it down to the failure of his own mission.

"I found the troops who attacked the Tourville, and if only I'd had the resources to take them on, maybe we could have…"

"Colonel Taylor," said Irala.

He looked to Lasure first to see if he had anything to say, but the Admiral wouldn't look him in the eye. Taylor couldn't work out what was going on. He expected some ridicule and consequence for his failed operation, but this was an entirely different and disconcerting experience. So he turned to Irala, who was the only one who wanted to speak to him.

"Colonel Taylor. You should never have been allowed to travel to the location of the ambush of the Tourville. Admiral Lasure did not want you to go and knew it was a dangerous risk, and an unnecessary one."

Taylor couldn't believe what he was hearing and could not understand where the hostility was coming from.

"Colonel Taylor, you must submit to the authority of the chain of command," added Irala.

Taylor was shocked. He couldn't help but feel that Irala was sounding more and more like one of his superior officers all the time, and not one of the good ones. Taylor felt his defences come up, and he lashed out.

"I've always done what I thought was best for us all. I went out there to do some good. It wasn't a failure, but we paid a heavy price, more than we can afford. Not every operation can be a perfect success. This is war."

"And neither of our people can risk losing a single life carelessly."

"I'm sorry, but what the hell is going on here?" Taylor demanded, looking over to White and Lasure.

White looked away. It was clear he didn't approve, but neither did he feel it was his place to say.

"Your command structure has proven inadequate to present the results necessary to win this war," said Irala.

Taylor ignored the alien and kept his eyes firmly locked on Lasure.

"What is going on here, Admiral?"

"I…I have given over command, overall command… to Irala and his people. They will coordinate our combined forces from now on."

"What? What the hell did you do that for?"

"You brought us into this war, Colonel," added Irala, "Now we are making sure we prevail."

Taylor couldn't believe what he was hearing. He liked Irala, but he had not seen this coming.

"You can't do this," he said to Lasure, ignoring Irala entirely.

"It is done," replied Lasure in a defeatist tone.

"Did they force this on you?"

Lasure shrugged.

"Well what the hell does that mean?"

"Colonel?" Irala asked.

Taylor could see he wasn't getting anywhere, so he finally turned to face the alien.

"Okay, tell me what the hell is going on!"

"We want this war to succeed, Colonel. Now that we are in this, we will not risk any asset more than we have to. I have taken command of the war efforts. A Marshal, if you will."

Taylor shook his head.

"No way, that's not how this works."

"Yes, it is now, Colonel. You will submit to the chain of command."

"Or what?" he asked aggressively.

"This has to be done, Colonel," Lasure interrupted, "We have a genuine chance here. Irala and his people are so far ahead of the human race, and we need their help. I've thought this through, and I believe it is the best course of action for us all. This isn't about ego or responsibility or anything else. This way we stand the best chance of winning, isn't that you want? Isn't that what we all want?"

Taylor couldn't believe what he was hearing. He could feel his blood boiling, and he knew he had to get out of there before he did something he shouldn't.

"This won't work, and it can't last," he said, turned, and stormed out. Barclay stayed behind, but Jafar followed close by as usual.

"Colonel Taylor!" Lasure shouted as he headed out the door.

"Leave him be," replied White.

Taylor stormed out. He could barely breathe, and he could feel his pulse racing. His heart was pounding, and he felt the temperature in his head building. Then he began to feel sick.

"This is not what you wanted?" Jafar asked.

"How can it be what I wanted? How long have we fought to be free? I go away on one mission and come back to find we've given it all up."

"But you like Irala and his people?"

"Yeah, and I like you, too, but I wouldn't pin stars to your uniform and start taking your orders…no offense."

"Why would that be an offense?"

Taylor shrugged and then nodded in agreement.

"Glad to know someone's head is in the right place."

Jafar looked confused as if he had no idea as to what Taylor meant. Silva strode into view, and Morris was close by his side. They could see the distress on his face.

"What's up, Colonel?" Silva asked.

Taylor barely knew how to explain it for a moment, but finally the words rolled off his tongue.

"Lasure just gave away everything we have worked for."

"What do you mean?"

He looked at Morris. "He's given command of our fleet over to Irala."

"What? Why?" Silva asked.

Taylor shook his head.

"Well you did elevate the Captain to that position of authority."

"What's are you saying, Morris?"

Morris sighed as if he was insulted by the prospect of having to explain himself.

"He's your monkey," he began, "You elevated a lowly ship's captain to the head of the fleet, the overall commander of the entire free peoples of the human race. Then you left him to manage it all. Not so surprising he turned to someone else, is it?"

"You've got a point," he muttered.

"What was that? The great Colonel Taylor admits he might have been wrong?"

"I wish I wasn't, trust me, Morris."

Taylor began to pace back and forth, and once again found his temper was beginning to get the better of him.

"How could he give it all away so easily?" he asked himself, "How could he be so stupid?"

Finally, he came to an abrupt standstill and found Silva blocking his path.

"You're not gonna fix this today. It's been a long day for all of us."

Taylor took a deep breath of air and tried to calm himself.

"What do you suggest?"

"Few beers. Relax and think about all this overnight."

"Just as well."

As he headed for the bar, he realised just how exhausted he really was. His first thought was to go right for his quarters and climb into a warm bed with Eli. But then it hit him like it always did. Imagining a world without her was impossible, and yet it was a reality for him now. He had nowhere to go. He didn't even feel like anywhere was home anymore. He was starting to hate the foreign world they inhabited, but his own bed felt lonely. Above all else, he wondered what was even drawing him to Earth now. He knew there was nothing left for him there.

He took a seat at a table not far from the bar, and it seemed like half the personnel there were greeting him and singing his praise. It all sounded like kissing ass to him, but he knew it wasn't. Captain King sat down and seemed remarkably cheery.

"What the hell is up with you?" he asked.

"You don't know?"

"This thing with Irala taking over, right? What's the

problem? He's a total badass."

Taylor shook his head. "Never thought I'd hear you say it."

"What? Accept that we need a little help. I'll take it and go along with it if it gets the job done, and gets us back on our own turf."

"But will it?"

King looked puzzled, and Morris sat beside them as Taylor carried on.

"We still don't truly know these people. Let's just not give too much away, more than we can afford to lose."

With that, he necked his drink and headed on for bed.

A single drink?

He imagined how Eli would rib him for being such a lightweight, and it brought a smile to his face. Within minutes, he was in his bed and passed out. It would have been the best sleep he had gotten in years, were it not for all the thoughts that swirled around his head.

As he dreamt, his imagination took him far from the face of Eli until he saw the pain and destruction of all he had witnessed. Lastly, he imagined himself in shackles with Erdogan's hands wrapped around his throat and squeezing the life out of him. Suddenly, he snapped out of the dream and awoke dripping in sweat. It was a horrible experience, but it only hardened his resolve.

Taylor leapt from his bed and pulled on his uniform. It felt awful as he was so filthy, but he was single-mindedly focused now, and nothing would delay him any longer. He rushed out of his quarters to find the sun was only just in the sky. Early enough that Jafar had not even arrived as his escort yet. He had no weapons and no gear at all. He rushed out into the open area of the desert where he had been shown to the Aranui base below.

He turned and looked around in all directions. There was nothing in sight as he expected.

"Irala!" he shouted.

There was no response.

"Irala!" he screamed at the top of his voice.

He turned and turned, looking for Irala, and then as he made a third full turn, the alien stood before him.

"What can I do for you, Colonel?"

Taylor took a deep breath and calmed himself before finally opening up.

"You know this won't stand?" he asked.

There was no response.

"I can't let you take control, you realise that, right?"

"It is the logical course of action if we are to win this war."

"Logic? Yeah, not really my strong point. Passion…is. By doing what you're doing, you are crapping all over what we have fought for and what we have achieved."

Irala seemed intrigued and waited for Taylor to continue.

"We haven't just fought these wars for survival. We fought them for freedom, freedom from all those who would try and impose their controls and values upon us. And whatever your motives, you have to understand we need to do this ourselves. Stand with us. Stand beside us and fight with us, but don't try and rule us. We fought for the right to rule ourselves, and you fought and survived for the same. We don't want to rule you, and we don't want to be ruled over. Can you understand how vital our freedom is to us?"

Irala thought for sometime before answering.

"Even if that would lessen our odds of victory?"

"Even then. Some victories just aren't worth the cost."

"My people may not feel the same way."

"Then that is their choice, just like this is ours. Lasure never had the right to allow you to take charge, and you should have known better than to take him up on it. You know what it is to fight for your freedom, and you would do anything to keep it. So how can you wilfully take it from others?"

"We can lead this war better than your Admiral or your generals can."

"Yeah, but we're human. It's not about the best road to take, but the one we choose. Let us do this."

Irala slowly nodded in approval.

"I will, but I cannot guarantee my people will continue to support you if you take this course of action."

"Then let's cross that bridge when we get to it, agreed?"

He reached out his hand in friendship, and Irala took it.

CHAPTER SIX

Taylor stood in the operations room once again, with Lasure and Irala either side of him. Both looked to him to act, and both looked uneasy. General White sat across from him and just nodded in approval. Six other high-ranking officers stood around them, but they all waited for Taylor to speak.

"First things first," he finally stated, "Our command structure is a disaster. Admiral, I understand the pressure I put you under when I elevated you to this position. You've done a fine job so far, but let's get you a little help."

Lasure looked relieved to hear those words.

"General White. I want you to assume command of all matters human that take place on this world. We need division of command between what happens with the fleet and what goes on down here. You okay with that?"

"Surely am, Colonel. I'm sorry to say that I am still in

no fit shape to go to war."

"Managing our resources here is just as important as managing them in the battle for Earth. Lasure. I need ground commanders, Army and Marine brass that can coordinate what goes on when we start operating on a larger scale. I know we have plenty amongst the fleet. If they've not already been brought into the fold, do so. We need them on board."

"And you, Colonel?" Lasure asked.

"I've interrupted and meddled enough. I can't promise I won't again in the future, but I am a combat officer first and foremost. I need to be out there where I can do what I do best. And while that is my job, I cannot coordinate and manage resources, and nor would I want to. I have one purpose left in this war. You all know what it is, and I do, too. Point me in the right direction, and let me tear them down piece by piece."

"And when you are not out there fighting?"

"Then I will work as a military advisor here," he replied and turned to Irala.

"Your input is always appreciated, and I am glad to call you friend."

"Then you will not mind if I propose our next target?"

"Fire away."

But Lasure interrupted.

"Gentlemen, I have already discussed these plans with Irala, and I have many duties to attend to. I will be returning to the Diderot if you want to reach me."

The Admiral left and all looked to Irala for the next potential target. Irala pressed a few keys on a control device on his arm and a projection displayed before them.

"This military installation houses several thousand Mech warriors, but it is also has a factory that repairs and builds military craft."

"They've got that kind of operation up and running already?" Taylor asked in amazement.

"That's Volgograd," said White.

Taylor looked amiss, as the name meant nothing to him.

"A town of heavy industry. All they've ever built there are tanks and other heavy hardware. It's the perfect site."

"You say thousands, how many are we talking about?" asked Taylor.

"Five or six thousand, we believe. They are housed mostly in two areas of accommodation beside the factory," Irala added, pointing to two areas that had around twenty tower blocks each.

"So they just took up residence in the factories and accommodation already there? They certainly aren't wasting anything."

The room fell silent as Taylor looked over the 3D projected map and all its detail. He passed over warehouse after warehouse, stopping when he found a district that was walled off and had towers every fifty metres. It looked as large as one of the accommodation districts that the

Mechs were using, although the buildings inside were just two storeys high.

"What is that? A prison?"

"Yes, for the slaves that assist at the site."

Taylor's face scrunched up as he tried to understand what Irala meant.

"Slaves? What slaves?"

And then it struck him, and his face became stark with sadness.

"Humans?"

Irala nodded.

Taylor turned to Jafar who had said nothing.

"Do they do that? Use other races this way?"

Jafar nodded. "Sometimes. They lost many in the war. They probably need human workers more than ever."

"Who are they?" he asked.

"Anyone strong enough to work. Soldiers, labourers."

He looked back to Irala, the horror showing on his face.

"You knew about this? Why didn't you mention it before?"

"Because we have seen you make brash decisions and act before you have thought it out."

"You're damn right. How many are in that camp?"

"Hundreds, maybe thousands. We do not know for certain."

"And you were just going to leave them there to rot and not tell us?"

Irala nodded without a second thought as if surprised that Taylor would have thought any differently.

He took a deep breath and looked at the map again, remembering how he felt when they freed Jones from an enemy facility. He began to feel sick in his stomach as he realised how many they had left behind.

"I never thought they would keep our people alive," he muttered.

"Demiran would not have," added Jafar, "But Erdogan is smarter and would not waste a resource."

"A resource? Is that what you think they are?" Taylor howled, as if in pain.

"To Erdogan they are."

"Well not to me!"

"Okay, Colonel, this is emotional for us all. Let's keep a cool head, and see if we can't work this out," said White.

Taylor tried to take longer breaths and calm down as he looked at the map once again. He could see a large oval building that was open topped. It was not far from the complex and appeared to be a stadium. It seemed to be brand new and was not of human construction.

"What is that?"

"An arena," replied Jafar quickly.

"For what?"

"To fight."

"For what? Sport?"

Jafar nodded.

"Yes, and entertainment, punishment, sacrifice."

"You're trying to tell us they're putting humans in there?" White asked abruptly.

"Yes."

Taylor shook his head in despair. He knew he shouldn't be surprised by the news, but it still disgusted him just the same. He turned back to Irala who was as calm as ever.

"You didn't tell us about this for a reason. I understand why, but that is not how allies work. You've told me how valuable your people are to you. How would you feel if I knew where some of your people were being held captive and forced to fight it out for entertainment? How would you feel if I knew that and didn't tell you because I didn't think I'd like the way you'd react to the news?"

Irala's head tilted slightly before he looked back to the prison displayed before them. It was clear to everyone that he had not given the prospect a second thought.

"We should have told you, but it would be foolish to attempt to rescue those prisoners."

"Maybe, but that's our decision to make. We're allies. We can't keep this kind of stuff from one another, okay?"

Irala nodded reluctantly.

"So, what are we going to do about this?" Taylor asked them all.

"We must attempt to destroy the facility and as many of the Krys as possible, but we cannot risk a rescue attempt," stated Irala.

"Why?"

"Come on, Colonel, you know why. The last rescue of human prisoners was a disaster, and you know it."

"You don't need to remind me, General," Taylor spat back.

"Clearly I do! The operation to rescue Commander Kelly and his people was green lit because you forced the issue. It resulted it not one human soul saved, and at a great cost to you personally, to the fleet, and to all of us!"

"We were drawn into a trap, and that was my fault, General, but is that a reason to give up on the rest of our people?"

"I think you need to start thinking with your head and not your heart. This operation will be hit and run. We will not have the time and resources to free a few hundred or thousand prisoners, and be sure they do not pose a threat to us."

"We can find a way."

"Do you think it's fair?" White asked, "Fair to ask our people to risk it all like this?"

"If I may," Irala interrupted, "You're thinking small scale, Colonel. It is your greatest weakness; that you first look to saving one, a hundred, or a thousand. We look at the entire picture, as I believe you say."

"Yeah? And what is that?"

"That saving one hundred of your people will save just one hundred of your people. Win the war, and they are freed along with all others."

"If they live long enough for that," he replied.

But he knew what Irala was saying, and he gave it some serious thought. He looked to the General for a second opinion.

"I hate to say it, but he is right. We're not ready for this yet. We go in and strike where it hurts them most, and then we get the hell out."

"Those people locked up in there, how long do you think they have?"

White shrugged.

"And how long do you think it will take us to win this war?"

White shrugged again as he rubbed his chin and avoided the question.

"That's what I thought - no idea."

"This isn't a matter of choice," Irala said, "We have selected a target that will damage the enemy most, while risking as little of our own resources as possible. This is the primary target, although we have selected nine more secondary targets that will be attacked simultaneously."

Taylor looked shocked.

"You can't win this war on your own, you know," General White said quietly.

"And they're all like this?" he asked.

"Strategic enemy targets, yes."

"With human slaves?"

Irala nodded.

"My god, there must be thousands, tens of thousands."

"And when we're ready and able to help them, we will," said White.

He turned to Morris who he could see was looming in the background as usual and had been listening. Taylor beckoned for him to come forward.

"What do you think, Captain?"

"It's not my place to get involved in operational decisions. I shouldn't even be here."

"Bullshit," replied Taylor, "I shouldn't be here making these kinds of decisions either, but that's the way it's gone. So let's hear it. Weigh in with your thoughts, and let's see if we can't come to some sensible conclusion."

Morris paced cautiously up to the table and looked around to see they were all looking at him. There was nobody except him below the rank of Colonel, and yet Taylor's introduction had given him a level of authority he'd never known.

"Speak up, Captain," said Taylor.

Morris coughed to clear his throat and finally spoke in a quiet and reserved voice.

"When I first heard there was a chance to rescue Kelly and so many of my friends, I jumped at the chance. But the reality was a sobering experience. I'd not want to leave a single human being to the mercy of Erdogan, but neither could I ask any one of those who fight with us to risk another disaster like we saw so recently. I do not believe in good conscience that we can succeed in this mission without losses that we cannot afford."

Taylor was amazed to hear it, but it seemed to mean so much more from coming from Morris.

"Even if Kelly and the others were in one of those places? Even if you could confirm they were there?" he asked.

"Even then, Sir. We have to focus on winning this war, and not letting our emotions cloud our judgement. You care more for those under your command than any officer I've ever known, Colonel, but sometimes that leads you into rash and dangerous decisions."

Taylor looked to Kelly for final confirmation. He simply nodded.

"Okay. Then we hit these targets and that's it. When do we go?"

"Forty-eight hours," replied White.

Taylor looked unimpressed.

"Why wait?"

"Come on, Colonel, you need some time to rest, as does everyone else. Equipment needs repairs and maintenance. New crews must have additional training time to get acquainted with crewmembers and equipment. We simply all need time."

He looked back to the fight arena still displayed.

"It's the one thing we don't have a lot of, General."

"That's where you're wrong. We've got a solid base here. We do have the time. What we don't have are the manpower and resources to throw away. Most of all, we need men and equipment on the top of the line. You think you are going to kill Erdogan?"

"Damn right," he snapped.

"Yeah, well how do you think you'd fare against him if you left in a few hours' time and met him on this mission? How do you think that would pan out?"

Taylor was silenced.

"We need you at your best, Colonel. We need everyone at their best. Forty-eight hours. We'll meet at 0900 hours to discuss operational details. Until then, get some R&R. You deserve it."

He left and strode out with Jafar and Morris close at his side.

"You are going to accept this?"

Taylor looked at Jafar in surprise.

"Why wouldn't I?"

"Because you always do what you want."

Taylor laughed, an experience that had been all too infrequent lately.

"I don't like what we have to do, leaving those people there, but it doesn't change the fact that you are right, and so is Irala. We must look at the bigger picture."

"And you're okay with that?" Morris asked.

"Not really, but we can't always have what we want.

Let's get the mission done right, and we'll be a step closer to getting them back."

They continued on to a covered staging ground where they found their Regiment all sitting about casually, cleaning their weapons and doing other maintenance. King sat at the head of them with his rifle half stripped on the table and his body armour in a heap on the ground nearby.

Not one of them moved when they saw Taylor approaching. They were all too intimately familiar with each other now that none of them cared for formality. Taylor knew they'd do anything he asked, and they knew he'd do anything for them.

"We got a job?" King asked.

"You make it sound like we're gonna hit a bank," Morris grinned.

"Bank? What the hell would we do with money?"

Morris shrugged, realising it was a fair point.

"Listen up!" Taylor called out to everyone.

No one got up, but they all turned their attention to the Colonel.

"Well done on that last mission. I know it didn't really go to plan, but you kept it together, and we got back home. Or what is home right now. We have been given a forty-eight hour respite. I will hold an operational briefing at 1200 hours tomorrow. Sergeant Major, I'd like you to oversee recruit training, and see if you can find a few replacements that meet our standards and can be brought in. The rest of you, aside from tomorrow's briefing, your time is your own!"

Cheers rang out around the shelter.

"Easy to please this lot," King said.

"They earned it, and it's easy to forget what good a little time off can do."

"Yeah. Not sure you'd know, Sir."

Taylor was stunned by the Captain's tone, but before he could get a word in, King continued.

"Join us. You haven't taken time out since Parker died. I know it sucks, believe me, I know," he said, holding up his hand that showed his wedding ring.

He'd never spoken of his wife, and Taylor had never thought to ask. He felt ashamed for not having ever inquired. He sat down before the Captain, and Jafar and Morris flanked them.

"You're right, and I'm sorry."

"For what?"

"For your loss."

"Yeah, well shit happens to all of us. But she'll never be gone. Parker. She'll always be up here if you want her to be," he said, pointing to his head.

"I'd like to think so," replied Taylor, "So your wife, what happened?"

King took a deep breath. It was obviously a difficult subject for him.

"Killed in the first war. You know we were in Rome

when the first invasion came, on vacation. By the time we knew what was going on and tried to make it back home, it was chaos. After a few days, I managed to get a ride on a civilian transport heading for South America. Cargo of expensive cars aboard and heading for some billionaire in Brazil, can you believe it? Pilot said the guy wanted to get them out before the war really got going, as if it was never going to reach him that side of the water."

"Not so crazy when you think about it. When has a war ever consumed the world quite like this?"

King shrugged, and they all listened intently as he continued to tell the story.

"I put a gun to that pilot's head and told him to dump the cars on the strip. Loaded up almost a hundred Americans who were trying to get back home like us, me and my wife. Lots of them had come from the embassy there. We got out of there before any of the fighting reached the country, and we thought we'd made it."

He paused for a moment as he had visions of it flooding back into his mind, and he came close to tears.

"We were over the Atlantic and on the home run when we were hit. First impact took out two of the engines. Second blew a hole right through the fuselage. We lost a few dozen through that breach before we lost enough altitude. Some friendlies engaged whatever attacked us, and we never saw either again. We thought even then that we might make it. But the power to the remaining engines soon failed and flight controls were fucked."

He reached for a canteen of water and sipped from it as they all hung on to his every word.

"Pilot put us down best he could, but we pretty much dropped out of the sky. Flotation pods kept the wreck up for about fifteen minutes, but she was a goner. The crash killed the pilot and maybe another thirty or so aboard. Eighteen of us made it on the rafts. Distress signal was put out, and we just had to wait, couple of hundred miles off the coast at least. It was then I realised the clamminess of my hands as I held her - Catherine, my wife. Blood, pouring out quicker than I could stop. A piece of debris had punctured her back and gone right through. All the training in the world, but there was nothing I could do to safe her. Couple of minutes was all we had left together."

"You can't blame yourself for that," said Morris.

"Believe me, I don't," he replied confidently, "I know exactly who was to blame for it, just as you all do. But we can't go on living in a perpetual state of misery. I'm gonna get revenge for Catherine's death. I've had a fair share of it already, and I'm gonna go on living as she'd want me to do as well. So believe me, when I say I know how you feel, and I know how to deal with it."

Taylor nodded in agreement, and he felt humbled.

"So will you take some time to relax with us, and enjoy the time we have?"

He knew he couldn't refuse, no matter how he felt.

"You have any children, you and your wife?" he asked.

"We had a son. Signed up to be a Ranger on his eighteenth birthday. That was two years before the invasion. After the war started, I only ever saw him twice more. He died defending New York."

"Hard fighting there," Taylor said quietly.

"Hard fighting all over. If it weren't, we wouldn't be out here. We've all lost a lot. Not one of us here who hasn't lost a loved one. Plenty of us have lost everyone we share blood with. Ain't nothing we can do but pick up a rifle and go forward. Keep living, keep fighting."

"Do you think we can win?" Morris asked him.

"Of course we can. If we don't think we can, then we have no hope."

"It's one thing to know you have to believe in winning to achieve it, another thing entirely to believe in what you preach."

"I don't believe it is," said Taylor, "You either believe it or you don't."

"So we're gonna win?"

"I can't tell you when or how, but yes, we're gonna win," said King confidently.

"And say we do. What will we do when this is over? What will any of us do?"

Nobody answered Morris' question. It was hard to imagine a world without war now.

"I'm just not sure what any of us have got to go home

to. I have no idea if anyone I knew back home is still alive, not even my ex-wife, who I'd actually be happy to see now. What have any of us got?" asked Morris, "No family, no home, nothing. Not for any of us."

"We have our lives," said King, "It's the only thing that hasn't been taken from us yet."

"And we have Earth, the home that we can take back," Taylor said.

"But will it be the Earth you knew? The Earth you fought to defend? Or will it be a barren wasteland?"

"What do you mean?" King asked.

"Say we can beat Erdogan, you think he's gonna leave our world as he found it? And what about his armies? We can never go back to the way it was."

"We never can. We can never go back to yesterday, last week or last year, no matter how good or bad it was. Times change, people change, life goes on," Taylor said.

Taylor finally relaxed properly for the first time in weeks, and he knew he had Captain King to thank for that. He rested back in his chair and sighed in relief, feeling everything was going to be okay, but his mind soon wandered back to the mission they were due to undertake. He looked to Jafar. He sat motionless across the table from him as if waiting for something interesting to occur.

"Tell me more about these arenas."

"You are no stranger to the arena," replied Jafar.

"No, but I've never seen a Krys one before."

"It is the same, just more violent."

"So they fight to the death?"

"Often. Little to no armour and using blades."

"Blades? Just metal blades?"

Jafar nodded.

"It is a tradition many thousands of years old. Sometimes the fighters fight to kill, or until only one still stands. Sometimes it is an execution."

"Sounds all too familiar," he replied.

"What do you mean?" Morris asked.

"Just sounds a little too close to our own history, don't you think?"

"Yeah, but we gave it up a long time ago. We evolved beyond barbaric entertainment," Morris retorted.

"Until recently, anyway," added Taylor.

"But your arena fights weren't assassinations."

"Weren't they? Put me in a ring with your average Mech without any heavy weapons, how fair is that? Might as well leave them shackled and have me take their heads off with an axe."

"That was a mistake. Those shows," said King.

"I know," Taylor said wearily, "I knew then, and I still know now. They were bad times."

"What, and these are better?"

King shook his head.

"What?"

"You're still missing the point, Morris. We can't change

what has been and gone. All we can do is go forward. Right now we've got a little respite with friends, enjoy it for what it is. You want to change the world? Start going about it, and get your head out of the past."

Taylor smiled when Morris was brought to silence and pondered King's words, and he himself heeded them also. He rested back and put his feet up on the table. Just as he was getting comfortable, he heard a voice calling.

"Colonel Taylor!"

Ah, fuck!

He recognised the accent and looked up to see Coco approaching. He'd not seen her since the funeral service for all they had lost. Her face was taut, and she walked with intent as if on an important mission. She was heavily pregnant, but that wasn't going to stop her.

"What can I do for you?" Taylor asked, pulled a chair up beside him, and pointed for her to take a seat, but she stopped before him and remained standing.

"You're going to leave those people down there?"

Taylor shook his head. "I don't know what you're talking about."

"Don't lie to me. I deserve better. You're going on a mission to where people are being held prisoner, slaves. Forced to fight for their pleasure. You know it's going on, but you're going turn the other cheek and leave them to rot. Shame on you!"

She was absolutely irate, and yet she wasn't wrong. He

reached up and physically forced her down into the seat beside him and whispered back.

"Who told you this? This is vital mission information that should not have passed into your hands."

"It's doesn't matter how I got it. What matters, is you leaving those people to die. How could you? How could you leave them?"

Taylor shrugged. "It's just too dangerous, for us all."

"Too dangerous? That is not the Taylor I used to know, and not the friend Charlie loved so much. You know what he'd think of you if he was still alive?"

"He'd understand."

"No. He'd find a way, and so would you have. What's happened to you, Colonel? You used to care enough that you'd do anything to help those in need."

"I'm sorry, but I have to think about the safety of all of us, and not just those prisoners."

"The Taylor I used to know would do both. It is a sad day that you would shy away from helping our people."

"You have to understand, this is the best course of action for all of us."

He reached in to wrap his arms around her. She tried to resist and smacked him several times to the chest with hard strikes from the side of her hand, but he still pulled her in close as she began to cry.

"I'm sorry," she mumbled through her tears, "Just imagine if that were Jones in that prison. What would you do, then?" She was still wrapped in his arms with her head buried into his shoulder. Finally, she pulled back wiping the tears from her eyes and began to calm down.

"What would you do, then? Would you leave him there?"

Taylor shook his head. "Not a chance."

"Whoever is being held in those prisons, don't you think there are people out there who care about them as much as we did about Jones, and how much you care about all of these people?" she asked and pointed around the room, "They deserve your help the same as the rest of us. I don't care what your orders are; you have always found a way to do the right thing. Please don't stop now. Charlie admired you for your devotion to those you cared for. Do it for him."

He looked over to Morris. He had heard most of what she had said.

"She's not wrong," he replied.

"Twenty minutes ago you were saying we couldn't take the risk."

"Maybe so, but a pretty face can change a man's mind."

"Ain't that the truth," King joined in.

Taylor shook his head in amazement.

"So you two will back me up on this?"

Morris nodded.

"I don't even know the mission yet. But given the choice of rescuing a load of our own, and not, you know where I stand."

Taylor sighed.

"Damn it, I should have listened to my gut."

"If we can't do everything to help save our own people, what is it all for?" asked Coco, "And you know what Eli would say."

He thought he could almost hear her then.

"This is gonna piss a few people off. Our allies among others," said Morris.

"Shit, well they'll just have to live with it," said Taylor. He looked to Coco. "You have my word that I will do everything I can to get those people out, everything."

"Thank you, Colonel. Now if I may, I must rest."

He helped her to her feet, and she was on her way.

"That's one strong-willed woman," said Morris.

"Damn right."

"So what are you gonna do now?"

"I'm gonna say how it's gonna be."

"So much for not meddling."

Taylor leapt to his feet and stormed back to the HQ building. Only Jafar followed him this time. He was ushered through into the operations room where he found General White alone. He was going over maps, and a few assistants were working in the background.

"Back so soon?" he asked.

"Get me a line to the Admiral."

White didn't question the request even though it was

rather forceful. A video call opened before them to the bridge of the Diderot. Lasure was on the bridge and turned in surprise to see Taylor on screen.

"How can we help you, Colonel?" he asked.

"I thought I could let this go. I thought I could leave our people to suffer to keep us safe, but I can't, Admiral. A good friend of mine just reminded me what it is that makes us human, and keeps us human. I am sick of being the hunted. I am sick of leaving people behind."

"We've already discussed this matter, Colonel."

"I don't think you're hearing me, Sir. We're going to get those people out, and there's not one among my Regiment who would disagree with that decision, as I am sure the rest of the fleet will agree. We've had to compromise a lot in this war, and we've had to give up a lot. It's time that came to an end."

Lasure didn't know what to say. He looked around the crew on the bridge of his own ship, and they clearly were in support of Taylor.

"Do you think it can be done?" Lasure finally asked him.

"We have a chance. I know that."

"And the risk of losing it all?"

"Sometimes the risk is worth taking."

"Then you have my approval, Colonel. General White, please see that our allies are informed of the change in plan, and be sure they are ready to assist. Lasure out."

White looked at Taylor with utter amazement.

"How on Earth did you just manage that?"

"I appealed to his humanity. It's what we've got left, and can never be taken from us while we still draw breath, and that's why we're going after those prisoners - our humanity."

CHAPTER SEVEN

Taylor allowed himself to slip into a dream world inhabited with the fond memories he had of Parker. The R&R seemed to pass quickly as he spent much of it sleeping to rest up. He was aboard the Baron once again now and still dreaming of her when he heard his name being called over and over. Suddenly he felt something strike his helmet, and he snapped back to reality to find Rains had just given him a good smack.

"Still with us?" he asked as Taylor came around.

"Unfortunately," he replied.

Rains sat down beside him on benches in the docking bay of the frigate.

"Finally feels like we're at the beginning of the end, doesn't it, Mitch?"

"That a good thing?"

"It is if we win."

"Any particular reason you've picked this time to come and annoy me, Eddie?"

"Do I need a reason?"

"All right, Eddie. No, it doesn't feel like the beginning of the end. You know why? Because we're still not back on Earth for good, we haven't freed the however many thousands, maybe even millions of people enslaved there, and Erdogan still lives. So no, it doesn't feel like that at all."

But Eddie wouldn't be swayed.

"Come on, you miserable bastard. It wasn't so long ago that we thought it was over, and now look at us. On the road again and hitting Erdogan where it hurts."

"You're positivity is outstanding. I'm just not sure it's grounded in any facts," replied Taylor.

"And yet he's right," Morris said, "Stay the course. You've held us all together this far. We need you to the very end."

"I'll be here to the very end. I just wish so many of our friends could have been. Jones, Chandra, Friday. We've sacrificed and lost too much to lose now," he said.

He looked at his watch.

Fifteen minutes to go.

It was that awful wait before a big event, compounded by the fact they were never certain what they'd encounter on the other side of the gateway, no matter how much surveillance had been carried out. He looked out across the deck and the four copters waiting to go. Close to half their Regiment was waiting to embark for the assault. He knew that to call themselves a regiment was far fetched at best, but he still like the way it sounded, even if they were an independent company in reality. He liked to feel they did the work of a regiment.

He looked about the deck to see that half the faces were trained on him, waiting and hoping for some words of encouragement. He didn't feel enthusiastic at all, but then he turned his thoughts to Coco's words, and it inspired him to get to his feet. He looked at each and every one of them. There were so few left of those he had begun with at the start of the first war. But there was not a rookie amongst them.

"Thank you! Thank you for your continued support and confidence. You've never faltered or failed me, or the cause. You are the reason I am still alive and fighting today. We are about to embark on the biggest operation since we left Earth. Over ten thousand personnel, including five thousand ground troops and the largest fleet commitment we've ever mustered. This operation began as a hit and run attack, but has evolved into a complex operation the likes of which we never dreamed we'd ever experience again!"

He looked to Irala, or the projection of him at least.

"Our allies have given us an opportunity to win the victory that was stolen from us. Humans were born to live on Earth, and Earth is where we shall live, but until that time comes, we must preserve human life, wherever it is. We have selected ten targets for this operation. They will be hit simultaneously in order to maintain the element of surprise and create mass confusion and a division of enemy resources."

He took a deep breath.

"What you may not know is the reason for the escalation of this operation. There are humans at these locations. Imprisoned and made to work as slaves. Worse still, they are being forced into fights to the death for the enemy's pleasure and entertainment. I cannot tell you how many of our own we expect to find, but every single one that we get out of there is a victory in itself."

He could see the amazement in the faces of them all, but it soon turned to hope as they realised the chance they now had.

"We could come out of this with a few dozen POWs, a few hundred, or even a few thousand. We've got plenty of transports waiting to jump in to deal with whatever capacity we need. Once we hit the ground, we'll likely have a one-hour window. So let's do this. Let's get our people out of there!"

There was deadly silence while they all contemplated what they were facing, and stayed silent as they waited for the countdown. Finally, they were given the ninety-second countdown over the tannoy.

"All right, people, let's load up!"

The tone was solemn as they emplaned ready to begin the operation, and Taylor took his seat beside the cockpit as Rains climbed aboard.

"You know, Taylor, I don't how you are still alive after all you have been through. But what amazes me further is that I'm still here to fly you. You know what the odds are of me surviving all the bat shit crazy missions you get me in on?"

"What?"

"Zero, man, the odds are not in my favour anymore. Whatever power protects you, I ain't got. I don't know how many more of these missions I've got in me."

"Told you before, Eddie, you'll outlive us all."

"Yeah? What gives you that idea? Your friends don't seem to last all that long."

"You're one of them, and you're still here."

Rains shook his head as the final ten-second countdown began.

"Promise me one thing, Taylor."

"Anything."

"Promise you'll never leave me to them. I always come back home, or I don't come back at all, got it?"

Taylor was shocked to hear it. It was the most sincere and serious Rains had ever been.

"You got it."

"Three…two…one…jump."

Taylor and Rains watched the scanners in the cockpit.

It was a tense moment, waiting to see what they would come up against.

"Anything?" Taylor asked.

"We've got…shit…incoming!"

Taylor looked to the screens. Two large enemy vessels and fighter wings were on an intercept course.

"Guess they're getting a bit bored of us pissing in their back yard!" Rains yelled.

"It's our yard, and we want it back," replied Taylor casually.

The docking bay doors opened, and natural light flooded into the cockpit. The beautiful sight of Earth greeted them.

"Magnificent, every time," said Taylor.

"What do you want me to do? Some heavy shit out there."

"Stick to the plan. We go in!"

Rains put the power down, and they soared out from the hull of the Baron. As they made it out, Taylor studied every video feed on the screens around the cockpit. He could see beams firing from the Aranui vessels, and the Diderot's guns lit the ship up from bow to stern. Pulses from the enemy vessels were already pounding the friendly vessels.

"I sure hope they can handle themselves. They're our ride out of here," said Rains.

A wing of a dozen enemy fighters was closing fast, but

they could see the Baron and her support vessels were closing on an intercept course and had already opened fire.

"Should have a clear run at it from here," said Rains.

"Good."

"Volgograd, never been there."

"Me neither, Eddie, can't say I ever wanted to."

They were into the atmosphere in less than three minutes of arriving in the Solar System and soaring towards their targets. On the scanners they could see dozens of other copters and heavy support craft on their flanks, and they knew there were many more out of scanner range.

"Never thought I'd see it again," said Rains.

"What?"

"A full on assault. No pissing about, no guerrilla attacks. We're finally back to the big leagues," he stated as they watched dozens of their capitol ships duke it out with the Mech vessels defending the world.

"Let's see how they feel, hey? See how they like it."

As they got into orbit, they could see some of their allied fighters already cutting a path through enemy ships that had scrambled to oppose them, but it was too late.

"Jump was perfect. We're three minutes out from the target."

As he said it, they could see one of the enemy vessels get through their wing of fighters ahead, and Eddie was quick to target it with the nose gun.

"Time for payback."

He squeezed the trigger. The first few shots went wide, but he kept his finger down and simply directed the tracer fire towards the enemy ship. Several of the rounds smashed into the lower hull of the craft and tore off several of the guns fitted there, but it soon banked to make a pass and rushed past them. They looked back to the screens. It was banking hard at their rear and coming around for another pass.

"Sixty seconds out! He's coming up fast!"

Taylor took one last look at the screens before rushing to the side door where the enemy ship would soon fly past. He hit the door release and felt the turbulence as air rushed in. He raised his rifle and watched the enemy craft begin firing as it came for another pass. He took aim as it came up beside them and was about to pull the trigger when he heard Eddie yell.

"Incoming!"

Rains banked hard, and the pulse from the anti-aircraft battery below missed them by centimetres and just scorched one of the side doors. The marines were thrown about.

"Whoa, that was close!"

He looked back with a smile, but Taylor had disappeared. Jafar rushed to the doorway to just make out Taylor falling to the ground a way back.

"Oh, shit," said Rains.

Jafar leapt out without any further hesitation, though

they had already covered considerable ground by the time he had gotten out the door.

"Bring us around!" Silva shouted.

"I can't. We have our orders!"

"You want to be responsible for getting the Colonel killed?" Silva shouted.

"Hell, no!"

Taylor felt his thrusters kick in, but he was stunned. He remembered hitting something hard on his way out of the door and was just about coming to when he felt the ground beneath him. The thrusters landed him safely, but his legs gave out from under him immediately, and he collapsed like timber on the light snow beneath him. He felt his helmet crash into the hard surface of concrete beneath the light smattering of snow before he finally came to a standstill.

The impact on his head was enough to wake him up, despite the fact it sent pain surging through his neck and down his spine. He groaned as he put his hands out and pushed himself up until he was kneeling. The first thing he noticed was blood in front of him – human blood. It was not his, but it glowed on the surface of the snow. He looked up to see three humans.

One was cut and bleeding badly, one wore a dirty and torn set of fatigues, and another had nothing but a pair of ripped jeans. The third was a young woman who looked scrawnier than any of them, but she had blue blood splattered over her shoulder. They looked filthy and malnourished. They stared at him with wide eyes and utter astonishment. Each one of them held some type of close combat weapon. One had a spear, another a half-metre long short sword, and the third a metal ball ended mace. The weapons looked as if made with crude blacksmithing skills.

"Taylor," one of the men whispered.

He was in utter shock and had no idea what he was looking at. He looked past them and could see a two-metre high wall, and crowds of Krys sitting above them. It all made sense to him now. He pushed off on his right leg and stood up straight. He turned to see that he had landed almost dead centre in the arena. Hundreds, if not thousands of the aliens packed out the tiered seating around them.

One Krys lay dead at the side of the arena with a trail of blue blood leading up to him. More than a dozen human bodies were scattered about the floor. He stopped to look at the creature standing opposite the three humans. It didn't wear the Mech armoured suits he was familiar with.

The creature's head was exposed, but it wore a slim armoured plate on its torso and another on its right arm and right leg. Despite the lack of armour, it was the largest Krys he had ever seen, standing at almost nine feet.

"Oh, boy," he muttered to himself.

"It's really him, isn't it?" asked the terrified woman

behind him.

He looked up to the stalls to see that barely a single one of the Krys was armed or armoured. That was something at least. Finally, his eyes locked with the huge beast in the arena. It bared its teeth and appeared to growl at him. He simply smiled back and turned to the humans.

"Yes, I'm Colonel Taylor. I'm here to get you out, but I don't have much time. How many of you are there here?"

The woman looked astonished.

"You don't know?"

"Until two days ago I didn't know the name of this city and had no idea a single human was here. Quickly please, how many?"

"We were twenty-five thousand when came here. Now, twelve thousand."

Taylor's eyes lit up. The losses were horrific, and yet all he saw was the potential number they could save. He looked down and found his rifle had gone, his shield, too. Only his Assegai and his pistol remained. He drew out the blade and raised it in the air.

"I am Colonel Mitch Taylor!" He shouted for all to hear, but he need not have spoken so loud, as his voice was boosted through hidden microphones that amplified his voice around the entire arena.

"You know who I am, and you know why I'm here. I have been the cause of death for more of your kind than are sitting here today! Surrender, and I assure you that no further harm will come to you!"

No response came, until finally he could hear the massive creature in the arena begin to laugh. It was a slow and low down grunt of a laugh that amplified to almost deafening levels.

"Okay, so that's how it's gonna be," Taylor said to himself.

The creature raised its weapon into two hands. On one end there was a metre long blade and the other a double-pronged hook. It shouted out some words in its own language before charging at him like a raging bull. It swung for him with a horizontal strike so powerful it would have cleaved him in two. He ducked under and thrust his Assegai into the inside thigh behind its leg armour and braced for impact.

Taylor held on tight and firm as the creature connected with him, and he brought it to a dead stop as it cried out in pain. It raised its huge pole weapon up and thrust the hooks downwards like a pile driver, but Taylor was quick to spin out of the way and drive his blade into the small of the beast's back. It twisted around to strike him, but he simply ducked under to where had come from, and up under its torso plate into the stomach.

Blue blood gushed out from the wound and coated his lead arm. The beast folded almost in two and lowered its head to his level. He drew out his Assegai and drove it up under the creature's jaw, through its mouth, and right up into the brain. Further blood poured out over him. He stood under the wound as if it were a shower. He held it there for a few moments just for grizzly effect before drawing it out and stepping out from the creature. It collapsed lifelessly into the snow in a pool of its own blood.

Utter silence followed.

"It's really him," one of the men said.

The three of them hadn't moved from where he'd first seen them. The silence was finally broken by the sounds of large doors opening around them. He turned and looked all around him as the blood continued to seep from his skin and armour. Five Krys warriors stepped out into the arena. They were equipped with a variety of armour and hand weapons just as the first had been. None were quite as large, but they closed in on him until they formed a circle ten metres in diameter. They had walked right past the three other humans, and Taylor was glad of it. He could see they had suffered enough already.

Not one of the creatures made a move now, as if waiting for him to initiate. He seized his opportunity and rushed at one. His attack was so fast that the creature barely had time to raise its sword, but his first strike was only a feint, and he quickly ducked under and thrust his Assegai into the creature's groin, and then into its neck as it keeled over.

As Taylor regained his footing, he could see the other four were already descending upon him. They came at him in a line, so he dashed to the right flank and then kept moving so that he drew them into a column and nullified their numerical advantage. Now he only faced one creature carrying a very short spear and shield almost as tall as it stood.

As the creature lunged for him wildly, he leapt back with his lead foot and thrust down into the upper arm so that his Assegai went right through and immediately incapacitated the arm. He then took hold of the top of the shield with his left hand and forced it down, thrusting his Assegai into the creature's face. The blade went deep into the beast's left eye socket with no resistance at all, but before he could draw it out, a huge glaive descended onto his weapon. The Assegai was pressed against the shield and eye socket at each end. The force of the cut snapped it in two as he recoiled back for safety.

Taylor was left holding nothing but the handle of his broken weapon that was now rendered useless.

"Taylor!" one of the men yelled. He turned to the spear thrown into his hands, and twisted just in time to drop to his knees and drive the spear high. The tip pierced the throat of one of his attackers, and as it collapsed down on top of him, it ran down the length of the shaft. He let go of the weapon and leapt out as the other two descended upon him. He had gotten out of reach, and they began to circle him now and see that they had to work together. He stopped, and they came to a standstill, too. His hands were empty now.

He looked from one to the other and then back again. The one to his right carried a short sword, and the one to his left had two hatchet-like blades. They were standoffish and cautious now. They knew to attack together, and he knew he was in trouble.

"Come on, you fuckers!"

It was enough to draw them out. The second he saw movement out of the corner of his eye his right hand ripped his pistol from its holster. He got off two shots into the face of the sword wielder. He quickly turned to face the other, but it was too late. He voided away, but one of the hatchets clipped his cheek and opened up a deep wound.

He raised his pistol to fire, but the next cut from the other hatchet smashed it down and out of his hands. The creature came at him swinging wildly now, and all he could do was back off and void each of the strikes. Suddenly, he saw his opportunity to go forward and jumped into a roll below a cut coming for his head.

As he came back up to his feet, he noticed one of the enemy blades lying on the ground beside him. He grabbed it and was back on his feet in seconds and now stood against the last creature. With his left hand, he gripped the combat knife on his webbing. The creature let out a frenzied scream and then came right at him. He drew the dagger and threw it in one. The blade embedded in the creature's shoulder and gave him the opening he needed. The wound caused one of the axes to drop from the beast's grasp, and as the other cut weakly towards him, he stepped aside and brought down a heavy cut onto its wrist. It was severed and dropped to the snow still grasping the hatchet.

The Krys warrior stood before him now helpless, but he showed no mercy. He raised the sword up and cut down with all his power so that the blade drove deep into its collar and twenty centimetres down into its body before it collapsed down dead.

"My name is Colonel Mitch Taylor. If any of you make it out alive, you tell Erdogan, I'm coming for him!"

Taylor was breathing heavily, and he could taste the foulness of the blood on his lips that was now mixing with the salt of his own sweat. It was seeping into the wound on his cheek, but he refused to show any sign of weakness. He stood before them defiantly, now without a weapon in hand. Several of them began to rise out of their seats. He hoped they would turn and run, but he knew he wouldn't have so much luck.

A few leapt over the arena wall and descended in to confront him. They picked up the weapons of the fallen as dozens more leapt in to join them. The three humans bunched up with Taylor as he prised a hatchet from the creature's dead hand and got ready to defend himself. He knew he had no chance now.

The Krys warriors were all around them now and just ten metres away when explosives rang out in the stalls. He looked up to see automatic gunfire rain down on the creatures. Then he heard screams, and a hail of more gunfire as Jafar appeared from one of the doors that his attackers had come from. He was gunning the enemy down mercilessly. There was more gunfire, and marines began to descend from two craft above them. The Krys began scattering and running for their lives. He took a deep breath and sighed in relief as he turned to the three humans standing beside him.

"You really did it," said the woman, and she began to cry.

Taylor could see multiple scars on her body that had been inflicted over many months. She was no stranger to combat, and he didn't think any less of her as she collapsed into a heap at his feet and balled her eyes out. Her accent sounded eastern European, but he didn't know well enough to say where from.

"You all soldiers?" he asked them.

The two men nodded. Taylor looked past them and saw Silva descend into the arena with all who were aboard their copter.

"You're safe. I'm sorry it took this long, but you're safe now," he said to them.

Silva rushed to his side after taking a few shots and stopped to look at the bloody mess he was in.

"We left you for two minutes, what the hell happened?"

"Landed in a heap of shit is what happened."

"Your weapons?" Silva asked, looking at the hatchet in the Colonel's hand.

"Used 'em."

Silva drew out his Assegai and handed it to Taylor who then reached down and picked up his pistol.

"Always land on your feet," Silva said, smiling.

"Feet? Think I landed on my damn head."

He looked back to the three arena fighters.

"Can you stick with us until we can get you out?"

"We'd follow you anywhere," said one of the men.

He reached down and hauled the woman to her feet.

"You good?" he asked her.

To his amazement she was smiling.

"I am now," she replied.

He looked out across the stadium. The unarmed Krys were still trying to flee and were getting bottlenecked at every point. It was a turkey shoot, and not one of them felt badly about it. Even over the sound of rifle fire, they could hear the ship borne artillery and missiles hitting strategic locations all across the base. They could feel every impact through their feet from the ground reverberating. He turned to see Jafar approaching. Taylor looked back to console the three fighters with him.

"He's with us."

"We know. We all know Colonel Taylor and Jafar."

Taylor was surprised but glad to hear it. Jafar looked at the blood on him and the bodies scattered about.

"A good fight?" he asked.

"Well, I won."

"Good, then."

"I'm Ruzena," said the woman, "and this is Cyril and Rob."

"Not normally on first name basis with many," said Taylor, "but you can call me Mitch, if you like."

He could see in her eyes that they were all scarred deep down, like Jones had been. If using given names was what helped to keep them going and kept them human, he wasn't going to argue with it.

"Colonel Taylor, er Mitch," said the woman, "everyone talks about you. Prays for the day you'll come and save us, and here you are."

"Yeah, well I'm not alone, but we have got a tight window, so let's move!"

He looked at the map on the pad fitted to his left arm. The screen was cracked from an impact, but it was still readable.

"We're only half a klick from the prison," he stated.

They rushed out from the arena and saw Krys warriors fleeing in every direction. Almost none of them were armed, and they were being cut down from automatic fire from seemingly every direction. Taylor wanted to stay and enjoy watching their defeat no matter how sick it made him feel, but he knew he had a job to do. They hurried onwards. The two towers at the entrance lay in ruins, and several others were being hit from the air.

As they approached, a few Mechs rushed out from the building to confront them. Taylor stayed behind the lines of shields and watched his people systematically gun down what little resistance there was.

"Hey, Rains!" Taylor called into his comms.

"What can I do for you, Colonel?"

"Get us those transports, and plenty of them!"

"Yes, Sir!"

The gunfire stopped, and they kept advancing to the gates and passed through a section that had been flattened by aerial bombardment. Not one of them slowed down as they ran inside the first vast warehouse like building. It resembled a low roofed hangar.

Silva and Herrera were first through the entrance and were cautious, but Taylor merely strode through after them with the three arena fighters by his side. There was no resistance left. They came to a standstill. A line of human prisoners met them. They were all pressed up against a clear glass entrance. They were in near darkness until Jafar reached a console beside the door. He pressed a few keys, and the doors slid open and lights flashed on.

Taylor gasped as the room lit up. All they could see for hundreds of metres were human beings crammed in. Improvised bunks that were eight high had been built in narrow corridors through much of the building. There were thousands of people there.

"My God," said Silva.

"We've done it," said Herrera.

"Colonel, this is King, come in," he said over the comms channel.

"This is Taylor," he replied still in shock.

"We're in Building C. I don't think you're gonna believe this."

"I think I might."

If only Eli could be here to see it, he thought.

Dozens of the prisoners flooded out and swamped them. They couldn't stop thanking them. Taylor paced over to the console where Jafar still stood.

"This place got a tannoy system of some kind?"

He nodded in return.

"Put me on it, all buildings if you can."

He pressed a few keys and then casually nodded to say it was on.

"This is Colonel Taylor of the free human fleet. We're here to get you out, and to tell you that we're still in this war. We're on the road to victory, but first, we must get you to safety. Transport ships are arriving as we speak. Please be patient. We have thirty minutes to get you all to safety, so make your way in an orderly fashion to the western fences which you will find have now been destroyed. Welcome back to civilisation."

Cheers rang out that reverberated through the entire building. Silva patted him on the shoulder.

"I never thought I'd see the day that we'd get people back, not in this number. Look at them. You've given them hope."

"No, we have."

CHAPTER EIGHT

Taylor stood outside the prison entrance as the thousands of free prisoners passed over the downed fences. He could see a number of them were starting to ask where the transports were, and that only brought a smile to his face.

A flash of light erupted above them. One second there was nothing but a bleak open sky, and the next there were dozens of transport ships. He could see the look of utter confusion on many of their faces, and some even started to question if it was all a trick, but they were too desperate to not risk giving it the benefit of the doubt. Rains' copter came in to land nearby, and he rushed to the door. His mouth was wide open with shock.

"Jackpot," he shouted as Taylor approached.

"How much time do we have, Eddie?"

"Mmmm….uh…." he muttered, as he looked on at the thousands of people piling aboard the transports.

"Eddie! How long?"' Taylor raised his voice.

"I don't know. I just fly this thing."

"What do your scanners say?"

"Right, got you," he rushed to the cockpit, and Taylor climbed aboard to look for himself.

"Our fighters are a little busy to the south. The Baron has come in to orbit to support us from the west. She's taking a bit of fire but doing fine."

"So how long do we have?"

"Right now, I'd say we're about holding. Longer we're here, the more pissed off Erdogan is gonna get."

"How long, Eddie?"

"Notifications from the Diderot say we have incoming in fifteen minutes."

"Fifteen?"

"Hell, we expected a few hundred, maybe a thousand or so; look at what we got! Between all the sites we must have picked up well over fifty thousand souls. That ain't no lightweight operation."

Taylor looked out through the cockpit. The first two transports were full and shutting their doors, but over a dozen more were still loading."

"What can we do?"

"Nothing. Everyone knows what they must do and what the stakes are. We load until we're full or we run out of time."

He watched every second countdown on his watch.

When they reached the deadline, they still had more than a thousand people on the ground. Everyone knew they had met the deadline, but their was no sign of the enemy, so nobody mentioned it. As the last few vessels were loaded, Taylor finally gave out a breath of relief.

"Signal Lasure, and tell him we're getting the hell out of here. And be sure to let the Baron know, too. I don't wanna be left here."

"You got it," said Rains.

Silva was standing just outside the copter alongside Jafar.

"We got away with it, and still no major response after all this time. You think Erdogan is finished?"

"No, but he's spread thin, I should imagine," replied Taylor.

"What will he do now?" Silva asked Jafar.

"Try and rally support with the underlords, those who serve him and used to serve Karadag, Demiran, and the other High Lords of the Krys."

"Sure gonna take him some time," said Silva.

"The Fatihi, where is it?" Taylor asked, "The only ship we know that has jump capacity, and we haven't seen it in a long, long time. That makes me nervous."

"Will these other Lords support him?" Silva asked.

"If they believe he can win, yes."

"Then what?"

"Then we're in deep shit. Let's focus on the task at

hand and worry about that if and when it happens. We just secured our greatest victory since we were driven from this world. Let's enjoy it while we can," Taylor said.

"Taylor," a deep voice called out. He turned to see Erdogan walking beside the fuselage of the copter towards him. Taylor drew his pistol and fired two shots quickly into the torso, but they went right through. Experience told him it would be a hologram, but he'd never be so naive to assume it was every time. He looked all around for any sign of the enemy, but there was nothing, so he holstered his pistol and squared off against the enemy Lord.

"You continue to impress me, Colonel."

"Yeah, well you don't impress me at all," Taylor snapped.

"That is a shame. Were you to join me, I could give you more than you ever dreamed of."

Taylor shook his head.

"I already had that, and you took it from me. I'm here to take it back, and your head with it."

"You have been a formidable opponent. It will be a shame to kill you, but also an honour and a privilege."

"I'll make you a deal. Put a gun to your head now and pull the trigger, and I'll save you an agonising death."

Erdogan laughed. It was the same low tone wicked laugh he had heard in the arena. It was unsettling, but his hatred of the alien ran so deep he remained focused.

"You'll never have your Earth back. You and your Aranui friends will die a grim death as you attempt to do so."

"You know this tough talk intimidation stuff is really getting old. I'm going to kill you before this is over, and that is a promise."

Erdogan laughed once again. "Good bye, Taylor, until we meet again."

Taylor rushed into the copter.

"Have we run checks on all who have gone aboard the transports? Every single one without exception?"

"You got it, all came up clean."

Taylor shook his head.

"I can't tell when that bastard is bluffing anymore, Eddie. He's fucked us over so many times I'm just suspicious."

"And you're right to be, Colonel, but I think we did this one right."

He nodded in agreement.

"All right, then, so what are we still doing here?"

"Good to go on your word."

Taylor leaned out of the craft.

"Let's load up! Go, go, go!"

Just a few moments later they were lifting off the surface, and Taylor couldn't remember a time he was happier to be leaving. He loved Earth, but only the Earth he knew, without Erdogan. They made their landing aboard the Baron and watched as the transports made their jump before finally they could leave themselves.

"When you're ready, Captain," he said to Barclay over

the comms.

He half expected the engines to fail or to be hit by some surprise weapon that would keep them locked within Erdogan's grasp, but it never came. The countdown reached zero, and they made their jump.

"Maybe he's not as powerful as you think?" Silva asked Taylor.

"No," added Jafar, "You are right to fear him."

The first thing Taylor did now they were aboard the Baron was to find a shower and have his wound sealed. By the time they entered atmosphere of Ony, he was fit for inspection and looking respectable.

"Look at them," Rains said, pointing to the lines of high capacity transports that had put down on the surface with the thousands of rescued prisoners, "It's incredible."

"Yeah, question is, how many more are there like it?"

"Were we wrong to leave Earth, Mitch?"

"No," Taylor replied quickly, "We could never have made it there. Best case scenario, is we ended up like those poor bastards in work camps. We had to leave, and it's the only reason we were able to keep up the fight. If we'd not met Irala and his people, it would all have been over a long time ago."

"Then I hope they understand that. Can you imagine being left to the mercy of the Krys when we bugged out?"

"We did what we had to do."

"I'm getting a landing request to put down at new

coordinates."

"Where?"

"HQ landing Zone A," he said in surprise.

"Well? Do it."

As they came in to land, they could see that thousands of the rescued prisoners had gathered around the HQ complex where General White was addressing them from the top of a shipping container buttressed against the landing pad. Rains brought them in for a smooth landing, and they stepped out to a hero's welcome.

"It is thanks to Colonel Taylor and so many men and women like him that have made this possible. This operation was Taylor's idea, this rescue attempt, also his. Let's hear it for Colonel Taylor!"

His voice carried for a kilometre over speakers set up all over the camp. Taylor shook his head and sighed as White beckoned for him to come forward. He tried to hold his ground, but Silva pushed him forwards.

"Welcome all of you!" he said as cheers rang out in response, "If you survived this long under the reign of such cruel hardship, you are truly tough people indeed. We need you to keep being that strong. Over the coming weeks and months I want to see an end to Erdogan, and we will need you to help make that happen."

"Just give us a gun and point us in the right direction!" a voice from a nearby crowd yelled. He looked down for the voice but was met by the most surprising of sights.

Commander Kelly stood in the crowd about two rows back and was looking up at him in amazement. Taylor didn't know how to respond. He knew they had been scanned, and that as far as they knew it was really him, but it was a bittersweet sight. A friend had returned, but he would forever be the face that led to Eli Parker's death.

"Keep fighting, keep strong!" Taylor shouted to the crowd before jumping down and heading cautiously towards Kelly. He wasn't sure how to react to him yet. He wanted to feel relief that his friend had survived and been rescued, and yet he was still wary. His last encounter with what looked like Kelly was flashing back to his mind, and he felt a spark of pain in his head and neck as he remembered what it cost him. He looked down at his own hands and expected to see Eli's blood on them.

Slowly, he looked back up. Kelly was advancing quickly now with a huge smile across his face. He rushed to Taylor and wrapped his arms around him in friendship.

"You really did it. You really came back for us," stated Kelly.

Taylor was still uneasy and uncomfortable as Kelly let him go. Morris appeared by his side, and Kelly embraced him, too.

"I can't believe we're out. I can't believe any of this. This place, these things we are seeing. It's like a dream. Where is your fine lady, Parker?" he asked.

Taylor's face went to stone.

"You don't know?" Morris asked.

"Know what?"

He looked to Taylor and could already see he had struck a nerve.

"I see," he whispered.

"No, no you don't," replied Morris in Taylor's defence.

Morris took Kelly's arm and led him off out of Taylor's sight. Taylor couldn't be more grateful, for he couldn't bring himself to explain Parker's death to the face that he had seen cause it. Despite Taylor's despair, the whole area was alive with discussion. He looked around to people smiling and laughing as if all was well in the world, and that consoled him a little.

It was not long before the sun had gone down, and Taylor found himself with a drink in hand at the centre of the greatest celebrations that had taken place since they had reached the distant world. He sat alone and was deep in thought when someone took a seat in front of him. He looked up to see that it was Dubois.

"Sergeant," he said in recognition.

"I think we're passed such formalities," she replied.

She wasn't even in uniform but comfortable clothes.

"Coco," she added.

She sat and stared at him for a while, and he wasn't sure what she wanted from him, though he knew he owed her.

"Thanks."

"For what?"

"For pushing me in the right direction."

"Before you lost Eli you would never have hesitated to attempt a rescue of our people, no matter how dangerous. You lost your confidence in yourself."

He knew she was right.

"Well, thank you, anyway."

Her hands reached forward and rested over his on the table between them. Her hands were soft and warm, and it was comforting after feeling alone without Eli. But as he thought more about her and Charlie, he began to feel and overwhelming sensation of guilt and was uncomfortable. He pulled his hands back out from under hers and tried to sit back and pretend he felt nothing.

"It's okay, you know."

He shook his head as if to not know what she was talking about.

"You're as stubborn as Charlie was."

"What do you want from me?" Taylor asked abruptly.

"We've both lost the ones we love, do we not deserve some consolation?"

Taylor shook his head. He could see what she meant now, and it was just too soon for him, but he could see in her eyes how lonely and desperate she was.

"If you can't be there for me, be there for my son, Jones' son. He will grow up without a father now, and you are the closest thing that he will ever have."

He shook his head again. He could not bear the

responsibility.

"You owe him, and you owe me. Most of all you owe our son!" she said, raising her voice.

Taylor was shocked and stunned by the prospect.

"Will you not do this for all of us?"

"I can't," Taylor replied softly.

"Can't? Or won't?"

"I am no father. Even if I survive this war, what kind of father figure do you think I'd make? All I know is how to fight."

"And to love," she quickly added, "You loved Charlie as much as I did. You loved Eli, and you love those who fight beside you. Nobody can replace Charlie as a father, but you can honour him and respect him in doing this."

He thought on it for a moment. It was never a subject he had ever given any thought. He knew the child was not far from birth now. He thought back to Jones and what he might want, and as he did so, the more he realised Coco was right. Quietly, he gave his response.

"If I survive this war, you have my word that I will be there for your son. I can't promise I'll be good at any of it, but I will try."

Coco wept a little in relief.

"You don't know how much that means to me," she replied and leaned forward, reaching once again to lay her hand on one of his, "Thank you."

He still felt uncomfortable with her hand over his. It

reminded him of being with Eli, and so he just wanted to reach across and kiss her, and that made him sick to the stomach with guilt. He also couldn't help but feel he was dishonouring Jones' memory by even thinking such of Coco, and she could see that in his face.

"There's nothing to be ashamed of here," she whispered, "Little Charlie needs you. I need you, and you cannot go on alone."

He wanted to accept that, but it felt so wrong. He pulled his hand back and stood up.

"I promise you I will be there for your son," he stated formally, "but I cannot offer you anything else but my friendship."

He quickly knocked back the last of his drink and headed for the bar. It was a lot to take in. For all the responsibility he had ever taken on board in his life, this hit him harder than much of it. He knew Jones would want him to look after Coco and their son, but he'd been too engaged with the war to give them a second thought.

The music went quiet and groans rang out from many around him. He turned to face the podium where addresses had often been made to them. Tens of thousands of military personnel were gathered there, and all were silenced now as they could see the Admiral himself had climbed up top to address them personally. He had been given no formal introduction. Few could get close enough to see his expression, but Taylor was just a few rows back.

He could see the smile on Lasure's face.

"Congratulations to all of you!" he began.

Speakers were set up all around the site and carried his voice to every human on the planet, as well as into the ships stationed there.

"Because of your efforts, there are now more humans out here on this world and in this fleet than we arrived with. That's right. Our numbers have strengthened because of your efforts. It's been a long and hard struggle since we left our homes, but I want you all to know that we are making progress. We are winning this war, and time is on our side now. I'm here to tell you that all operations to Earth are suspended for seven days for you all to rest and enjoy yourselves. Because when those seven days are up, we go at the enemy stronger than ever. Relax, rest, and be ready!"

Cheers rang out as the Admiral stepped down from the podium, and the music started back up, but Taylor was one of the very few who wasn't delighted by the news. He pushed through the ranks of partying troops to reach the Admiral. Lasure's people let him through, and he carried on walking beside the Admiral.

"Colonel Taylor, quite the accomplishment you achieved."

"We did all right, but why are we stopping?" Taylor asked abruptly.

"Because we're working our people into the ground.

They aren't machines. You may be single minded in this matter, and I think that is at the expense of those under your command sometimes, Colonel. I will not send exhausted personnel into combat when it is not necessary,"

"Necessary?" replied Taylor sternly, "We aren't talking about a small task here, Admiral. We have to take our home back, and that won't be achieved by sitting around drinking beer and sleeping."

The Admiral stopped and turned to face Taylor head on and make eye contact.

"How many men and women under your command have you lost since we left Earth?"

"Too many."

"And how many of those losses have you replaced?"

Taylor sighed. "Not enough."

Lasure reached out and rested a hand on his shoulder.

"Look to your people, Colonel. See their spirits remain high and that recruits are brought in as quickly as you can. No good can come of running yourselves into the ground. We need you until the end of this."

He turned and left Taylor alone. He knew Lasure was talking sense, but he still didn't like it. On top of all that, he knew that time off would only allow him to dwell on the guilt he was feeling regarding Coco and the responsibility she had placed on him. Captain King pushed through part of the crowd and appeared before him with a drink in hand that he thrust towards Taylor. He had the same infectious grin that had spread across all who were there.

"Come on, Colonel, enjoy yourself!"

It was clear the Captain had gotten more than his fair share of drinks, but he was still standing, and his enthusiasm and joy were hard to avoid. Taylor finally smiled in response and took the drink. King led him over to a table where a number of their officers and senior NCOs had gathered. Silva raised his cup in recognition as they approached, but Taylor felt a tingle run up his spine when he saw Kelly sitting amongst them. The former MDF Commander leapt out of his seat when he saw Taylor. He knew Kelly must be nearing seventy years old now, but he looked fitter than ever and sprung up like anyone of Taylor's own unit.

He froze and thought of backing off, but Kelly continued onwards anyway and stopped right in front of him.

"I know what you have been through. Morris has filled me in. Words can't express how sorry I am."

"It wasn't you who did it," although his voice was vague and unconvincing.

"But it might as well have been. I failed by allowing my people and myself to be captured by the enemy. I cannot change any of that now. All I can do is give you my promise that I am with you until the end. I have already discussed it with my people, mostly former MDF and Becker and his people. We want to volunteer for service in the Inter-

Allied. I know it's a big ask. But every single one of us is trained and with combat experience expected of one of the Immortals. I want to give back what you have done for us. Let us join you and stand beside one another in the coming weeks and months."

Becker strode into view to join them.

"You want in on this?" Taylor asked him.

"We owe it to you, and we want payback same as you," he replied.

Taylor looked over to King and Morris who had been listening in throughout. Both nodded in approval.

"How long until you can be at full combat capacity?" Taylor asked.

"Arm us tomorrow and we're good to go."

Taylor thought about it carefully and back to Lasure's comments about their losses. He knew this was a valuable opportunity to gain hundreds of trained fighters for his Regiment.

"Just give us a chance, Taylor. You know we've got what it takes. We survived a long time down there. Even more significantly, we fought. We didn't hide and run. We fought back. We gave them everything we had to give, and it cost us dearly. Now we've got a chance to hit them harder than ever. We just need you to say yes."

"And you'd submit to my command?"

Kelly nodded. "Without question. Equip us and feed us, and I promise you will not be disappointed. We will earn the reputation your Regiment has established."

Taylor tried to think back further than the clone of Kelly and remember the man he really was. He had never had anything but the utmost respect for the man. He was the oldest combat officer he knew, and yet his age never seemed to hinder him, and the weight he had gained through working at a desk for so many years was long gone. All that was left was a hardened fighter and combat officer offering his assistance.

"Come on, Colonel, do it for all of us," whispered Kelly.

Taylor finally stretched out his hand in friendship, and Kelly quickly took it with a huge smile across his face.

"We'll take you in, Kelly."

"Tom," he replied.

Taylor looked confused, eventually realising that in all the years he had known Kelly, he'd never asked him his full name.

"Thomas Kelly," he added.

In hearing his name, it suddenly humanised Kelly over the clone Taylor had witnessed kill his friends, and he felt a great weight lifted from his heart and shoulders. He took a step back and raised his voice for all around them to hear.

"Thomas Kelly, I hereby give you a field commission in the Inter-Allied Regiment. From now on, you'll be a Captain in this Regiment, and you'll lead Charlie Company, who you will raise from those who fought alongside you on Earth."

Kelly couldn't believe what he was hearing. He looked up into the night sky in relief before finally looking back down to Taylor.

"You won't be disappointed," he replied, "Thank you."

"To Captain Kelly!" Silva barked.

His voice carried far, despite the music and cheering that shortly followed. The celebrations continued as they took a seat together to discuss the details.

"Kelly, being newly established, you'll be a support Company to get going. You'll also command the largest Company in the Regiment. I want you to choose your staff and platoon leaders personally. I'll keep Captain Morris with me as my second and liaison to your Company."

Kelly nodded in agreement.

"You've almost doubled our numbers!" King said.

"MDF forces in the Inter-Allied, though, Sir?" asked Lieutenant Matthews.

"Why not? We're already a bastard mix of everything else, US Marines, British Paras, and Rangers. We've got Welsh Fusiliers, and a few others from British Regiments I can't even remember anymore. We've even got German Marines now. Doesn't matter where you came from. We maintain a high standard, and if you can keep to that standard and follow my orders, then you're welcome among us."

"Yeah, and let's face it, we need the numbers," Silva said.

Two days passed where they seemed to do little but rest and lay about on the safe surface of Ony. The war seemed so far away when they couldn't hear or smell what war meant to them all. But on the third day Taylor awoke to find Irala waiting outside the door to his quarters.

Taylor stretched as he stepped outside and buttoned up the collar of his uniform.

"What can I do for you?" he asked.

"We have vital information on a build up of enemy forces," Irala replied calmly.

"What? Have you informed our commanders?"

"Yes, they are awaiting your arrival."

Fuck, Taylor thought.

He jumped forward into a stride towards headquarters.

King, Morris, and Kelly were all standing outside the building when he got there. They looked anxious and as if they hadn't been waiting long.

"Any idea what's going on?"

"No, but it can't be anything good, Sir," replied King.

He rushed inside to see everyone was waiting for him, and stern expressions filled the room. The three officers of his Regiment had followed him in, but he was surprised to see that Jafar was already inside and standing with White.

"Taylor, good, come on in," said the General.

He took a few paces forward and could see they were looking at some kind of blueprint projected on the table between them.

"What is this?"

"These are images provided by our Aranui allies."

Taylor looked carefully and could see that whatever he was looking at was of Krys construction. It appeared to be part of the surface of a planet that was not Earth.

"Where is this?

White pointed to Jafar to continue.

"This is the planet my people call 'Bursa'. It is the largest industrial world in the Tau Ceti system."

Tau Ceti?

The name cut deeply as he remembered their withdrawal from the fateful expedition there that cost the life of Chandra and so many others.

"What are we looking there for? I thought Tau Ceti was cut off since we destroyed the gateways?"

"Yes, unless you have access to my people's technology," Irala added, "After Erdogan's assault on this planet failed, we attempted to pursue his ship the Fatihi; the only vessel in his fleet capable of initiating a jump gateway, utilising technology stolen from us as you know."

"Attempted?"

"Yes, we pursued the Fatihi, but it moved beyond our grasp into the safety of this world, Bursa, and the large defences and fleet that protect it."

"So what are you telling me? That huge fucking monstrosity could open up a gateway here with a whole fleet anytime she likes?"

Irala shook his head. "The Fatihi was severely damaged after our last engagement and took refuge on the surface of Bursa."

Taylor sighed in relief, but that relief was short lived.

"This is where we get down to it," stated White.

"All right, let's hear it," he replied.

"What you are looking at, Colonel, is the remains of that ship, the Fatihi," said Irala.

Taylor looked more closely, but it appeared more like some giant city built onto the surface.

"The enemy has spent much time and work getting to understand and repair the jump engines that were fitted onto that vessel, technologically antiquated compared to what we possess today. The engines we used for such jumps used to require vast power and ships the size of the Fatihi, but what they achieved was no less impressive."

"Okay, okay, I get it. But what does this all mean?"

"Colonel," said White, "they're turning the planet into a jump gateway that can be activated and allow access to anywhere, anytime."

Taylor's jaw dropped as he realised what they were facing. Kelly pressed a few keys, and the blue print map zoomed out until they could see the world it occupied and hundreds of ships in its orbit.

"So this is what Erdogan has been doing all this time?" he asked rhetorically, "No wonder we're seeing such success on Earth. He's not getting any reinforcements.

Every time we hit him, he gets weaker, and he knows it doesn't matter. Why hasn't this fleet come through yet?"

"More ships join this fleet every day," Irala said, "but we do not believe they are waiting for numbers. We believe the jump gate is not yet working."

"How did you come to that conclusion?"

"We witnessed a trial run a few hours ago. They have come a long way in understanding our technology, but they're journey is not complete."

"So we're safe for now?" Kelly asked.

Kelly had imposed himself as far more than just an officer on Taylor's staff, but he was glad of his presence and knowledge.

"How long?" Kelly asked again.

"We believe they will be operational within two weeks."

Taylor's face turned to stone.

"Two weeks!" King shouted.

The room descended into chaos until White finally slammed his fist down on the table and pointed for Lasure to continue.

"Gentlemen, it seems we have just two options. Our mission up until now has been to kill Erdogan and seize control of his forces. That achievement has eluded us thus far. The choice we have is to continue that task, with the intention of completing it within two weeks, or, we focus our efforts on disabling this jump gate."

"It's no choice at all," said Taylor.

Everyone looked to him.

"Even if we can find and kill Erdogan in that time, are any of you happy with having all those bastards one jump away from being on our doorstep? So what if we take Erdogan down, and they don't like or accept what we do from there?"

"I have to agree with Taylor," said Lasure, "This threat cannot be left unchecked."

"Things a damn fortress, though," added Kelly.

"The simple fact is," said Taylor, "man for man, soldier for soldier, marine for marine, we are better than they are. But they have such vastly superior numbers that we cannot hope to win if we have to fight them all at once. If that gateway becomes operational, then Erdogan will have all the resources, armies, and fleets he will ever need to secure Earth for good, and our opportunity will be lost forever. And when he's content that Earth is rock solid, where do you think he will go next? No, we cannot let this stand. We must try and destroy that gateway before it becomes operational."

"I agree," said Lasure.

Everyone agreed, despite the fact nobody wanted to try and take on the monumental task of trying to achieve it.

"Irala, you say this could be operational in two weeks, could it be sooner?"

"Yes, it could be tomorrow, or a month from now."

"Then, Gentlemen, I'd love to tell you we can come

back to this tomorrow after some serious consideration, but I am sorry to say that leave is cancelled, and we do not leave this room until we have found a way to make this happen. "

CHAPTER NINE

Over twenty officers and other staff and allies had been sitting about the table for two hours now. Everyone looked weary except Irala and Jafar, whose expressions rarely seemed to change.

"So what do we do?" Lasure asked, "Which plan do we follow?"

"Can't we just open a gateway right on top of the target and throw a nuke through?" Taylor asked.

"Works for me," said White.

They all looked to Irala for a response.

"Sending ordnance through a gateway has led to catastrophic effect. We will never do so again. Any large weaponry that passes through a gateway must be manned by a conscious operator."

"Okay. It was a sound idea. So what do we do?" Lasure asked again.

"Hit them with everything," replied White, as he looked at the images displayed before them, "A diversionary force to draw as much of that fleet away as possible, followed by an aerial bombardment. Nuke the surface, and have ground troops on standby for assault should that fail or the device not be disabled."

"Ground attack? Who would be crazy enough to do it?"

"We would, Admiral," Taylor said without hesitation, "Give us two nukes, and we'll deliver 'em by hand if need be."

"It's not a very subtle plan, Colonel."

Taylor shrugged.

"We will provide vessels for the diversionary force, as well as a secondary force for ground bombardment, and Guardians to operate in support of Colonel Taylor," added Irala.

"You know that a force large enough to create a diversion is gonna have to be vast?"

"Two hundred vessels," said Irala.

"We can spare a hundred between us. Any more than that and we leave this world unprotected."

"We only need to appear to have two hundred. We have a way."

Irala didn't seem keen to expand on that, so Lasure simply nodded and took him at his word.

"Taylor, what do you need?"

"Get me those nukes and fast transport for two hundred men, and we'll get the job done."

"Colonel, prepare your people. We set off as 1300 hours. I'll ensure you have enough support on the ground to give you the time you should need, if it comes to that. With any luck, this can be achieved with aerial bombardment, and we can return to our work on Earth. All further information will be forwarded to you."

Taylor nodded and casually walked out at a relaxed pace as he thought it all over in his head.

"Seems a simple enough plan," said King.

"Too simple," replied Taylor, taking a deep breath and trying to make sense of it all.

"You think it's a trap?" Kelly asked.

"How can it be?" asked Morris, "The enemy probably thinks they have a nice little secret there in their home system. Why would they ever think we'd be looking there?"

"Because Erdogan knows us," said Taylor, "He knows how we think. Let's not forget these are the people who defeated our race and the Aranui, and currently inhabit and own both of our homeworlds. Give them some credit where it's due. There's something we're not seeing."

"Well why didn't you say so in there?" asked King.

"Because I don't know what it is, but this is just too easy."

"Easy? It's gonna be an absolute nightmare."

"The stakes are too high for Erdogan to risk losing this

thing. He knows the war on Earth hands in the balance. This is his lifeline. This one target is what guarantees him victory. How far would you go to defend it if you were him?" Taylor asked.

"Few hundred ships in orbit and a substantial ground defence network seems about right," added King.

"I hope you're right."

"My Company will be taking this mission. King, I want you to lead two platoons in support."

"And us?"

"Get yourselves geared up, Kelly; you'll be deployed aboard the Baron for the duration of this mission. You will defend her borders and be ready to assist us if need be. That okay?"

"Anything we can do to help."

It was a bizarre experience to have Kelly under his command, and he didn't know why he was asking if his orders were acceptable, but he couldn't help but still see Kelly as an authority.

"Do you think your people will be up to this?"

"We've had a couple of days of good food in our bellies and freedom. We're ready for anything."

Taylor stopped, and they formed a circle around him, waiting to hear their orders.

"You all know what you have to do. With any luck, we shouldn't even be needed for this operation, but experience shows us things don't always go to plan. If we are needed on the surface to complete this mission, it should be nothing more than a lightning strike. But let's be sure we're ready for anything. Full combat load outs, extra ammunition and grenades. Breaching charges for every three men, 50BMGs for every ten. Let's make sure we can handle whatever job lands in our laps, okay? I want the Regiment assembled at 1200 hours, ready for departure to the Baron."

He looked at his watch and realised they had just thirty minutes, just enough to grab his equipment and be ready for the operation.

Good, he thought.

He didn't need any more time to dwindle on the past and other troubles. He was focused now and single minded in his actions. He got to his quarters and pulled on his personal gear. A rack beside his bed was loaded up with magazines for his weapons and spare grenades. He stored twice a full marine's load out in his quarters, for he wanted to be ready at a moment's notice around the clock.

Taylor pulled open the door to his quarters and stepped out in full combat attire, dressed head to toe in Reitech armour, but he froze as he saw a distraction he had been glad to be rid of - Coco.

"You're going back to Earth?" she asked.

He shook his head. "You know I can't discuss operational details with you."

"But you're going to fight, aren't you?"

"Rarely a day where I don't."

"Just remember this," she said. She reached and took his hand and placed it against her heavily pregnant stomach.

"You have this to come back to. You remember when Jones was mad with bloodlust and suicidal. You know who turned him around?"

Taylor nodded.

"That's right, you. You did. You saved him from that madness. Remember that, remember the man he would want you to be. Don't throw your life away."

"I don't ever go out there trying to die."

"And neither did Jones after you brought him back from the darkness inside him. He gave up his life because it was the only option to save us. Don't throw yours away because you think you should."

"You think I suffer from survivor's guilt?"

He sounded offended by the prospect, but she was shocked by the question.

"No," she said with a smile, "that has never been your problem. You just don't know how to let go and let someone else take the reins. You don't have to fight this war singlehandedly."

"Maybe it's not that I can't let go, I just don't want to?"

"One day it'll all be over, you know. Life will go on without all this bloodshed and heartache. Can you live in that world? Would you want to?"

Taylor shook his head. "I don't even know anymore.

I feel like I was put in this life to do one thing, and I am doing it. If I make it out the other side, we'll see about that."

"Good luck," she responded.

Her voice was calm and considered, and it reminded him so much of Parker. He nodded in response before stepping past her and continuing directly to the Regiment that was formed up as he had requested. Kelly was fully equipped just as he was now, and it was a reminder of better days. It was the first time he had seen Kelly and not scowled as he thought of the clones' attack.

"Looking shiny," he said to Kelly.

"Thank you, Colonel."

Taylor saw a large ammo container not far behind them and leapt up onto it so that he could look out across the breadth of his Regiment that now totalled almost six hundred, more than it had in a very long time.

"The mission we are about to embark on is in many ways the most important task we have undertaken since our evacuation from Earth!" he declared, "If we fail in this mission, then our ability to retake Earth is over. Our safe haven here will likely be compromised also! If we fail today, the time we will have left can be calculated not in years or months, but in weeks. The simple fact is, we cannot fail. No matter what, we must destroy the enemy's ability to create a gateway, or we are finished! Remember that. No matter what it costs us. Each and every one of our lives is worth paying to accomplish this, for if we do not succeed, they are forfeit regardless. Are you ready for this!"

An inaudible roar rang out, and he knew it was time.

"Load up!"

Kelly was quick to approach.

"You think things are that bad?" he asked as they watched the troops emplane.

"They could be. Erdogan has been one step ahead of us throughout most of the war. We finally get a little ahead, and low and behold he's got something else working in the background. He's not like any of the Krys Lords who came before him. We underestimated him over and over, and it costs us dearly."

"But you think they need to know that?" Kelly gestured towards the hundreds of troops under their command.

"I've never been anything but honest with them. How can I expect them to follow me and have my back, if I am not one hundred percent honest with them?"

Kelly shrugged. "It's worked so far for you, so who am I to judge?"

"Tell me something."

"Anything."

"When you were captured by the enemy, what did they do to you?"

"Honestly? A few days are just blank. I have no idea. After that, we were moved to the factories from where we were rescued. By all accounts, we weren't treated half as bad as I would have expected."

"You were a resource, of labour that is. Erdogan doesn't waste resources. If he could convince whole armies from Earth to join him, he would."

"I heard he tried that in China. They turned him down. It was a slaughter. Since then, people have just put their guns down and surrendered. It's what I heard while locked up there, anyway."

"I always thought we faced complete and utter extermination. If I'd known slavery and servitude were an option, I might never have left. A slave always has the chance to rise up. A dead man does not."

"You regretting coming out here?"

Taylor thought about it for a moment before shaking his head.

"No. So maybe we could have fought back in a few generations time, but if we'd been defeated, it would have been over for us. But then we didn't know we'd find the Aranui, and they have been our saving grace. Without them, we might as well have laid down our arms and given up."

"I don't believe you ever could have. It's not in your nature. If you were the last man alive in this universe, you'd still be fighting tooth and nail to the very end."

"Probably."

Taylor climbed aboard and watched Kelly load up

with his people. He sat down and blanked out the rest of the trip. He was focused now on what they had to do. Thoughts of what would happen if they failed filled his head, and that hardened his resolve. He woke as he heard the countdown to the jump.

"You know I told you I could only survive so many of these crazy operations?" Rains asked. He sat behind as usual.

"Yeah, you told me."

"Well if I'm gonna go out, better it be on a big one like this."

Taylor looked up to see Rains was smiling as ever. Taylor shook his head, and it brought a smile to his face, too. "Nothing ever gets you down, does it?"

But they were interrupted by the countdown.

"Five, four, three, two, one…"

They passed through the gateway, and Taylor watched the screens, desperately waiting to see what was before them. A few moments later he could see hundreds of dots on their scanners where they had picked up the enemy fleet.

"What the hell?"

"What is it?"

Rains pointed to the screens.

"We've got about fifty ships on this operation, but look at the scanners."

Taylor looked down to see hundreds of ships displayed

on the scanners. Rains tapped a few keys and got into the exterior view feeds of the Baron. To their amazement their fleet had expanded massively in number. They could see several ships that were exact copies of the Baron, and many other vessels they knew well. Finally, they spotted two versions of the Diderot alongside each other.

"Holy shit," said Rains, "They've done it. They've projected holograms of whole ships, of the whole fleet."

"If only we had such numbers and didn't have to cheat it," replied Taylor.

"Don't need 'em. We got you."

Taylor ignored his comment and continued to watch the screens and wait.

"Come on, they're not biting," he muttered.

"Easy now, they'll come," Eddie said confidently.

"We're too far out. They can see it's a diversion. We should have jumped in closer."

"Any closer and it wouldn't give enough of an opening. Don't worry; they'll go for it. Few hundred ships turn up on your doorstep, you don't do nothing?"

"Sure hope so."

They both watched carefully, and finally they could see a few enemy vessels begin to move forwards.

"Here we go," said Rains.

"How many?" Taylor asked.

They could see only six ships from the enemy fleet heading their way.

"Come on, we need a hell of a lot more commitment than that."

Only the six vessels continued on towards them, and they knew it would be some time until they were in firing range.

"Gonna be a waiting game."

Taylor took a step back and slumped into his seat.

"Not going to plan?" Morris asked.

"We'll see."

Twenty minutes passed, and they were all growing concerned.

"The Baron will have a firing solution in less than two minutes," said Rains.

Taylor didn't move.

"What are they gonna do?" asked Morris.

"Give them the shock of their lives," replied Rains.

Another minute passed, and Taylor got to his feet and leaned over Rains' shoulder once again.

"Think those holograms will hold up to inspection?"

"You gotta look pretty darn close to see otherwise, and I think we'll have something rather more important for them to worry about soon enough."

"What's the range on their guns?"

"About the same as ours. Boy, are they gonna have a surprise coming their way."

They watched the screens from the Baron and could hear the sound of the guns powering up.

"Oh, here we go," said Rains, clamping his hands together as if he was about to watch a great show.

A beam of light burst past the corner of the screen from one of the Aranui vessels and struck one of the approaching ships. The beam cut deep through the vessel and was repeated a second time until the ship was torn in two.

"Damn they got there ahead of us."

The guns of the Baron flashed to life, and they were joined by dozens of other ships. A single burst of three pulses rushed out from one of the enemy ships, but they were silenced shortly afterwards as the unrelenting gunfire from the allied fleet tore them apart remorselessly.

"Hell, yeah!" Rains yelled.

They watched the enemy craft be hit by repeated barrages and beams until they were nothing more than floating hulks.

"Any movement on the rest, Eddie?" Taylor asked as the others were still celebrating the minor victory.

"Nothing yet. Wait, wait, they're moving."

"How many?"

"Oh, a good many. Three quarters of their number at least. Even more now, and they're coming for us all right. All we have to do is wait," he said and began to laugh.

"You realise it'll be a damn blood bath if they get at us?" Morris asked.

Fifteen minutes passed as they waited anxiously.

"Almost there now," said Rains.

"You really think it's worth all this?" Morris asked Taylor.

Taylor nodded. "All this time we've been here? All this plan, this trap?"

"Yeah?"

"If they had the kind of jump technology we gained from Irala, they would have been on top of us with everything they had by now. It's the only thing that is keeping the enemy from concentrating force against us."

"They jumped in against us before, from Earth, why didn't they hit us with those numbers then?"

"They underestimated our strength, and Irala believes the Fatihi was too badly damaged to jump again after their retreat."

"So we were saved simply because of that one stroke of luck?"

"Hardly luck, was it?" asked Taylor.

"Almost there!" Rains hollered.

Taylor opened a comms channel to the bridge of the Baron.

"Send the signal, Captain."

"Sending now, Colonel," he replied.

"How long until the fleet is in range?"

"Three minutes."

"Then I hope they are quick."

They watched the screen from one of the surveillance

drones that had first documented Bursa. They could see almost twenty ships remaining in orbit over the planet, including one capitol ship. A light flashed nearby, and a gateway opened. From out of the opening came thirty allied vessels including five of the Aranui. They came out firing and had blown two of the enemy destroyer size vessels apart before they could turn to face this new threat.

"Good luck, boys," said Rains.

They watched the battle ensue like they were watching a movie, and they were powerless to act. In just thirty seconds, the Aranui vessels had broken through the enemy lines and had begun bombarding the surface while the human vessels duked it out with the Krys craft. The ships on both sides were pounded by repeated shots, and Taylor couldn't believe their vessels fought on.

"We've got incoming!" Rains called out.

Taylor looked to the huge fleet descending on their position and back at their fleet to see the holograms were gone now. They were severely outnumbered, and they all knew they could not afford the losses.

"We gonna go or what?" Rains asked.

"We can't, not yet. Takes too much power for the jump engines. We can afford one jump in all this, and one to get us back home."

The Baron's guns opened fire, and it was only seconds later that they felt the impact of pulses on the ship herself.

"Oh, I don't like this."

Taylor felt the same. They could feel the vibrations through the craft as the undercarriage of their copter was rocked.

"This ain't how it's supposed to be, Colonel. I'm supposed to fly, and you're supposed to shoot, and right now we ain't doing either."

"Just hold on, and stick to the plan," replied Taylor.

He looked to the screens to see the full strength of the enemy guns was being brought to bear now. The Aranui vessels had opened up with their devastating beam weapons but were being swamped by Mech vessels, and in amongst the enemy craft Taylor could see heavy assault craft heading their way. Barclay came over the comms.

'We can't take much of this, Colonel."

"Just stick with it for another sixty seconds. Tell Lasure to be ready to jump to Waypoint B on my command."

"Aye, aye, Sir," he replied.

Taylor knew it was bizarre for him to be giving the fleet commanders orders, but it was the way it had worked out, and he was okay with that. He turned back to the action taking place over the surface of the planet and could see their own ships were just beginning to get the upper hand, but at a heavy price. He raised a comms channel to Barclay again.

"Prepare to jump, Captain."

"You said sixty seconds, Colonel."

"To hell with that, jump, now!"

A few seconds later a ten second count down began, and he and Eddie watched the screens with bated breath. Pulses were smashing into every ship in the fleet, and they could see that boarding craft were less than a minute out from reaching them.

"Oh, this is gonna be tight."

"Five, four, three, two, one." The jump gate opened, and their fleet quickly passed through and came out just two klicks from the battle over the surface of Bursa."

Taylor didn't have to say a word as every single one of the ships in the fleet trained their weapons on the planet's defence force and opened fire. He could see a handful of enemy craft had managed to pass through the gateway with them, but the Diderot and her support vessels had already turned to face them.

"Get me a view of the surface," said Taylor.

Rains pressed a few keys and had it on screen almost instantly.

The display showed a scene of absolute carnage. The ship that had become a landmark on the surface looked like it had been opened up like a tin can. Fires ranged across multiple decks and beams from the Aranui vessels continuing to cut in deep to its core.

"They've done it. They've ripped that bitch apart," said Rains.

"You think so?"

"Look at it."

Barclay appeared before them on a display screen.

"Colonel, target is destroyed. We'll be ready to withdraw in nine minutes."

"Cutting it a little fine, don't you think?"

"We should make it just fine."

Taylor looked back to the displays to see the enemy fleet they had left in the lurch had already come about and were heading their way.

"It can't be this easy."

"Looks like mission accomplished to me," said Barclay.

"Humour me, Captain. Run surface scans on Bursa."

"If it fits into the window we have, you can have anything you want, Colonel. What do you want us to look for?"

Taylor shrugged.

"No idea, just look for something. Energy signatures from the jump engines we use. Any other objects that match the size and description of the Fatihi, anything."

Barclay looked surprised, but he turned to his crew and passed on the order.

Two minutes passed as Taylor merely watched the battle ensue. They had a huge advantage against the few ships remaining in orbit and were making the best of it, but he could see the rest of the enemy fleet was closing all the time.

"Colonel, we haven't found much of note," Barclay finally announced.

"Tell me what you have got," he replied.

"All we've got is a small energy signature on the far side of the planet. It's not much, and it's coming from an empty canyon. Just about one of the few parts of the damn world that hasn't been built on."

"What is it?"

"No idea, Sir."

"Take us around. I want to be sure."

"Sir, with all due respect, the target is destroyed, and we must remain with the fleet."

"Get me a channel to Lasure directly, and in the mean time, get us moving and continue scanning that area."

"Yes, Sir."

"What you expecting to find?"

"Hopefully nothing, Eddie."

Lasure appeared on a screen beside Barclay soon after.

"Admiral, we're picking up energy signatures from the far side of this planet that are related to the gateway technology. I am requested permission to take us around and investigate."

"You do what you have to do, Colonel, but you have less than seven minutes to do it. You don't leave when we do, and you're on your own."

Taylor acknowledged and looked to Barclay who immediately relaxed the orders. Taylor kept a keen eye on the time and watched the seconds pass by in between watching the screens of the battle.

"We find anything here, what do you expect to do about it?" Rains asked.

"Something," he replied sternly.

It took four minutes for them to come about and get into visual contact with the location Barclay had identified. As they did, they all looked at the screens and tried to make out what they were looking at. There appeared to be a huge round doorway cut into the surface of the canyon. It was larger than the biggest vessels in the fleet and was obvious to the naked eye, for it was the only smooth surface on the canyon floor.

"What the fuck is that?" asked Rains.

Taylor looked over to Lasure who was still on screen.

"Are you getting this, Admiral?"

"We are. What the hell is it?"

Irala suddenly appeared before the Admiral as a hologram.

"Colonel, we believe you have identified the location of a gateway built deep into the surface."

"Guess they're monitoring our channels then," muttered Rains.

"Wait a second," started Taylor, "You're saying that's the gateway? Not the Fatihi?"

"We have been analysing data collected from your vessel, and we believe a permanent gateway has been build one kilometre below the surface utilising the remnants of the engines aboard the Fatihi."

"And you only found this out now?"

Irala nodded as if completely missing his sarcasm.

"Well what the hell are we supposed to do about it? Can you take it out?"

Irala was shaking his head.

"That far below the surface and protected by thick blast doors, it must be destroyed from inside. We have identified a maintenance opening inside the canyon that you should be able to access."

"In the time we have?" asked Taylor in amazement.

"You have to try, Colonel. All our lives depend on it," said Lasure.

Taylor shook his head in amazement, but it was all the time he needed to think. "Open the docking doors and prepare to launch!" he yelled.

"Think you can put us down on top of that maintenance entrance, Eddie?"

"Flying you there is no problem at all, but I can't guarantee we won't get blasted out of the air by whatever defence systems they have in place."

"Our sensors show us that all localised weapon systems cannot target vessels flying at thirty metres below the surface."

"Thirty metres?" asked Taylor.

Rains gasped as the docking bay doors opened.

"Can you do it?"

"Oh yeah, sure, just as easily as I can get my head blown

off, Mitch."

With that, he put all power to the engines, and they rushed off the deck and out into space. They were already in low orbit and broke into the atmosphere quickly. As soon as they were through, they found pulses rushing towards them, but Rains was already in a dive to get under the guns.

"This better work!"

The surface was approaching fast, and yet he showed no signs of slowing, and the other copter pilots were following his lead. Finally, as it looked as if they were going to plummet into the ground, he lifted the nose and kept half power to the engines and half to the hull thrusters. They levelled off just in time and came to within five metres of the craggy surface that was so jagged and coarse it would have clawed the hull open if he'd pulled out just two seconds later.

"Damn it, Eddie, trying to get us killed before we've even started. Let's not forget there's a nuke on board, okay?"

"Ain't none of it gonna matter if we don't live to ram it down the bastards throats!" he shouted enthusiastically.

Taylor looked at the clock. They had just two minutes left.

"No way we're gonna make this, Admiral," he said to Lasure.

"You just do what you got to do, and we'll do the same."

Taylor looked back to the maps, and they were coming up over the canyon of the location they were heading for.

"Ain't nowhere safe for us to hang, just gonna have to put down," said Rains.

"Visors down!" Taylor ordered. He pressed the button on the side of his helmet, and the visor slid down and latched onto the neck ring of his suit.

Rains took them right over the vast circular entrance doors in the canyon and landed them on the far side. They put down hard and bounced a little before coming to a standstill.

"Everyone out! Move, move, move!" he yelled

They rushed out to find a quiet sight. The entrance to the gateway was just as it looked, a single huge round entrance in the surface itself that was made up of two halves that locked and connected in the centre. He looked at his Mappad and then up to the canyon edge to a well-hidden entrance. It was just as Irala had said.

"There it is, go!"

They rushed up to the cut in half way up the canyon face, but as they reached it, he looked at his watch. The time was up. He looked up to the sky and half expected to see the battle raging above them, before remembering they were on the opposite side of the planet.

"They can't last long up there, Colonel," said Morris.

"I know."

They rushed into the entrance, and sentry guns opened

fire on them immediately. Taylor raised his shield and took one impact before leaping back around the canyon entrance. His shield was smouldering from the burning hot impacts.

"Couldn't just be easy, could it?" he said to himself.

He pulled out two grenades, armed them, and threw them down the entrance. He waited until the blasts rang out and then rushed around the corner once again. One of the sentry guns was destroyed, but the other still fired on him. From the cover of his shield, he advanced and kept up the fire until one of his shots hit the barrel of the gun as a pulse was bursting from its tip and blew the gun apart.

As the smoke cleared, he could see they had come up against a huge thick armoured door that was three metres wide.

"Bring up the charges!"

They placed eight charges on the doorway, all close to one another. An explosion rang out as they were set off, and Taylor could see that all they had achieved was a small impact on the surface.

"What else have we got?" he shouted.

No response came.

"All the other charges you've got; bring me everything!"

They set the charges and took a pace back and waited for the blast. The impact rocked the ground, and it felt as if the cave were going to collapse, but as the dust settled, they could see a slight buckle in the door and nothing more. Lasure appeared on the comms. A fire was burning in the background, and he could see blood on the Admiral's head.

"Colonel, we can't survive much more of this. Whatever you're gonna do, do it fast!"

"We can't get into this facility, Sir. We need larger explosives!"

"Taylor, we've lost four vessels in the last minute. We cannot wait. Set the nukes and get the hell out of there!"

Taylor froze for a moment, as he tried to find some way to save the mission but was soon met by Rains, and he had no better news.

"Colonel, we've got incoming fighters and several hundred Mechs inbound on the surface. You can't stay there!"

"Fuck!"

"This is over. Let's save ourselves while we still can," said Silva.

Taylor couldn't believe he was going to accept it, but he had no choice.

"All right, arm one nuke here. Lang, see that the other is placed and armed at the centre of that gateway. We'll pick you up on the way past."

"Will it have any effect?" Silva asked.

"We can only hope."

"Armed and ready to go," a response soon came.

"Okay, let's move!"

Taylor led the way and sprinted back to the copters, taking up position with his rifle as they all got aboard. Finally, he climbed in but left the door open.

"Tell the others to go. We'll get Lang en route!"

The engines fired up, and he could see the other copter pilots eagerly lifting their birds off the ground and rush back towards the atmosphere to escape the enemy world.

"You sent him out there alone? Poor bastard."

"Just swing by and grab him, Eddie!"

Their copter soared over the gateway entrance where Lang was punching in the codes for the nuclear weapon.

"Come on, Sergeant!" Taylor hollered as they hovered just off the ground nearby. At last he turned and rushed back towards them, but as he reached the door, a volley of pulses struck his position and hit him in the back. He collapsed into Taylor who hauled him aboard.

"Go!" Taylor screamed.

Rains lifted off and put all the power down to see them once again racing back for the Baron. Taylor turned Lang over. There were three pulse impacts in the back of his armour and another in the back of his helmet. Not one had penetrated through.

"You lucky fucker," said Taylor.

Lang slumped down into a seat nearby and looked stunned. Taylor quickly made his way to the cockpit and watched in horror as they broke orbit. The scene before him was utter carnage. Several Aranui vessels had been completely destroyed, and many more of their own vessels floated lifelessly in space. Several human bodies bounced off of their cockpit. The battle was still raging, but it was clear they had paid a heavy price.

'My god," said Rains.

"Land us, quickly!"

"I'm doing it. I'm doing it!"

They rushed towards the Baron, but just as they were about the start their landing approach were struck by two heavy pulse weapons.

"I've lost power to engines! Life support is out! Flight controls are...limited!"

Nobody said a word as they watched and prayed that Rains could get them back home alive. They were approaching the landing area far too fast. Eddie was using all the power he could get for the forward thrusters, but it wasn't enough. They were off course and smashed into the docking bay entrance. They slid through and crashed into the landing area before scraping across the surface and smashing into the far side bulkhead. Taylor hit the comms channel a second after they stopped moving.

"All aboard. Jump!"

The countdown began, but they could still feel impacts hitting the Baron as the docking bay doors shut behind them. Taylor slumped down onto the floor of the copter and prayed they would make it. He could feel the gravity shift they had become accustomed to, and it was all the confirmation he needed.

"We made it!" Rains said.

Taylor got to his feet and looked around. No one had suffered anything but a few bruises.

"Yeah, we made it, but we failed."

CHAPTER TEN

Taylor sat at the bar with a drink in his hand. He still wore his armour, and his rifle was slung at his side. The dust and dirt from Bursa clung to his armour and his face where he had wiped the sweat from his cheeks with the back of his dirty glove. He hadn't even bothered to take his helmet off.

Lines of stretcher-bearers passed him as crews from the ships were ferried towards the hospital that had been established on the surface. The Diderot lay where it had crash-landed half a kilometre in the distance, with crews going back and forth. Kelly came to him first, as no one else could find the courage.

"You okay, Colonel?"

Taylor nodded as he took another drink.

"Oh, yeah, I'm just fantastic," he replied, watching another heavily damaged vessel come into land, and fires still raged on several levels.

"We fucked up. I fucked up."

"You can't put this one on yourself," Kelly quickly responded.

"Yeah? Doesn't matter whether I do or not, we're in deep shit."

Kelly laughed, and that made Taylor look up.

"Now we're in deep shit? When haven't we been? I think you're forgetting the war we're in, Taylor. We're in a war we should never have stood a chance in from the beginning. And yet, here we are, soldiering on."

"You saw the power of their fleet and the resources they had, how can we stand against that?"

Kelly shrugged.

"We'll find a way. You told me we could end this war by killing Erdogan, right?"

Taylor nodded.

"Has that changed?"

Taylor shook his head.

"No, just now we only have the time it takes for them to get that gateway working to accomplish such a monumental task."

"All right, then, let's do it."

Taylor was silent.

"Don't give me that silent treatment bullshit. I've had enough of that off others to last a lifetime. You are Colonel Mitch Taylor, and you don't give up. You can't. You have no right to after all this. What would Parker think?"

Taylor leapt up from his chair and swung a punch at Kelly that rocked him and made him stagger back before recovering his balance. Blood seeped from his split lip, but he made no attempt to return the favour.

"You don't get to talk about her. You killed her!" Taylor screamed at him.

"Is that what you think? And the clone of Jones, do you blame him for the deaths that clone caused, too?"

Once again Taylor went silent. He knew Kelly was speaking sense, but he was so distraught that he could not make sense of any of it.

"Almost a day has passed, and you're still wallowing in this shit," said Kelly.

Irala appeared before them without warning, as he often did.

"Great, you come to have a go as well?"

Irala shook his head.

"I am sorry, Colonel."

"For what?" Taylor asked, not understanding.

"The casualties inflicted on our people were too severe yesterday."

"What are you saying?"

"I am here to inform you that my people will have no further part in any combat operations that take place outside of this world. We will continue to give you refuge and help in any way we can, but only here."

"You're abandoning us now?" he asked, although he didn't sound too surprised.

"I told you my people could not afford to lose lives. Yesterday was the most severe loss of life for my people since the Great War. They will not fight anymore. Only I will continue to be at your side."

"You? Just you?"

"My grudge with Erdogan goes far deeper than my people's. I will see him dead even if it costs my life."

Taylor nodded, but it was hard to be enthusiastic after having lost their greatest and only ally.

"You have to try and change their minds. We need them," he pleaded.

Irala shook his head.

"Their decision is final. They will no longer leave this world."

"We're fucked," Taylor muttered.

"We've thought as much before. Hell, we've seen a lot worse," replied Kelly, "If there's one thing I know, Colonel Taylor of the Inter-Allied is never down and out. He's always in the fight, he's always got a plan, and he never gives up. Are you still that man? Are you still that marine, Colonel?"

He had struck a nerve, and Taylor stood up in defence of himself, and that only brought a smile to Kelly's face.

"So what do you suggest we do now? We have maybe two weeks, but that could be days or months. What do you propose we do?"

"What we should have done a long time ago. You keep saying it, and we get distracted at every turn. Find Erdogan and end his life."

"You say that, and I say that, but it never works out that way. Every time we get close, he seems to slip away from us."

Kelly looked around and caught sight of Jafar lurking in the background.

"Get over here!" he ordered.

Jafar paced casually up to them.

"Sergeant. You must understand Erdogan better than any of us; you served his kind for much of your life. How can we find him?"

"We've been through all this before," Taylor said in a weary voice.

"Yeah, well maybe it's time we tried it again, and again until we get the result we want," said Kelly.

He turned to Jafar for answers, but he said nothing.

"You must have something to add?"

"If I had any idea where to find Erdogan, that is where I would be now," he finally replied.

A path opened up ahead of them, and Lasure came through. He was heading right for Taylor, but he didn't get up. The Admiral stopped just two paces from him. His arm was in a sling and his head wrapped in a bandage. He said nothing as he waited for Taylor to say something.

"I had to try," said Taylor quietly.

"Of course you did. That is all any of us could do. It was worth risking all that we had to accomplish that mission."

"And yet it achieved nothing."

"Actually," Irala interrupted, "I have studied data from the blasts, and I believe you have delayed the enemy's progress on their gateway by up to two days."

"Great," Taylor answered sarcastically.

"We can't go back there. We don't have the strength for a second attempt."

"Then what, Admiral?" Taylor asked.

"You said we had just two options, and one of those is now beyond our reach. You have just one task, one order left to fulfil. You already know what that is."

Taylor shook his head. "I get it. I know what you all want, but I don't have the answers. I don't know where Erdogan is any more than the rest of you. Believe me, I'd give anything to know."

"Well you sure won't find him moping about here."

Taylor frowned at the concept that he was moping about anywhere and stood up before the Admiral.

"You have the full resources of the fleet at your disposal, Colonel. Every man and woman working in service of this fleet is behind you now. What do we do?"

Taylor shook his head and sighed. He didn't have a clue, but at least now there were no distractions. He looked back to Jafar.

"Erdogan would never go anywhere without a sizeable entourage of his most elite troops, right?"

Jafar nodded.

"Right, then. We've been hitting strategic targets of industry and his supply network, but we've never found the boss himself there. We need to know where his most elite fighting forces are deployed, or housed, and hit them."

"That's your plan?" asked Irala, "Hit random high profile targets in the hope you'll find Erdogan?"

"You got a better one?"

Nobody said a word.

"Irala, do you still have access to the surveillance drones in our Solar System?"

"I can provide you everything we have done previously, except the lives of my people. They will help you while it does not involve leaving this world and this system."

"All right, then. Find me a location. Better still find me many. Look for places that are lavish, and where the elite would reside; the sort that Jafar was when he was still one of them, the type of exclusive place that only the best of the Krys could expect to reside. They have a rigid class system, so they can't be hard to find."

"Can't be all that easy to attack either," Kelly joined in.

"You forget that until that gateway is operational, we still have the element of surprise. The enemy fleet over Earth has been dwindling throughout this war. Earth is weak right now, and Erdogan knows it. We have a small window to exploit that weakness before our world is lost to us for good."

General White was approaching from behind the Admiral and pushed his way to the front.

"Looks like you have some plan coming together," he stated.

"Just as Kelly says. Let's do what we should have done a long time ago. Let's kill the bastard!"

He stopped; realising dozens of officers and troops around them had stopped to listen in.

"If Erdogan gets the reinforcements from Tau Ceti, then this is over."

He turned to Irala.

"I don't care what your people think, once Erdogan has that technology working and the armies of his people rallied, he will come for this place; and all the technology and wonders in the world won't save you from his wrath."

Irala clearly agreed with him, but it was clear to both of them that there was no reasoning with them.

"What are you thinking?" White asked.

All eyes were on him now. They all looked for Taylor for the answer and would accept whatever he had to say.

"All or nothing. We might only have a week left to try and find Erdogan. I say we jump back to Earth with every fighting man, woman, and vessel we can muster. Everything."

"And the civilians?"

"They'll be safe here, Admiral, under the protection of the Aranui, and if we don't go, they'd be lost anyway."

"An all out attack?" asked White, "We've barely started hit and run attacks. Yes we've been successful, but you're talking a whole different ball game."

"You're damn right I am. Erdogan knows what a danger that jump gateway presents to us, and he also expects us to expend our resources trying to destroy it. He wants us to break our forces over that target, and then he'll mop up the survivors at his leisure."

"And you think risking it all is the only way?"

Taylor stood up and stretched before standing tall amongst them.

"So far we've never put more than a few thousand troops on the ground, but we have hundreds of thousands at our disposal. We probably have close to a half of what he has on Earth now, and we can choose when and where we strike. The only thing stopping us hitting with everything we have got is the fear of what we have to lose, but it's clear now that in another week or two, we'll lose it all anyway. Right now the enemy's armies are spread across the globe. We hit multiple targets on many fronts all at once, and we hit them hard."

"What if the Aranui are wrong about that gateway? What if the Krys are years away from getting it working again?"

"They haven't been wrong yet, and do you want to take that gamble?"

White shook his head.

"Hey, I never wanted any of this. I was born to fight, not to lead, but I can see we're on a gradual path of destruction. We have the chance to decide our fate now, and in a week or two's time it can be over, one way or another."

"What do you think?" White asked Lasure.

"I have heard no better suggestions. The enemy fleet orbiting Earth is modest. If we arrive in force, we can destroy that fleet and take control of the system. Then it's down to the rest of you to get the work done on the ground."

White looked to Jafar.

"One last time, Sergeant, will killing Erdogan end this?"

Jafar nodded. "Lord Erdogan is the leader of the Krys people, the High Lord. The one who kills him will take his position, or be allowed permission to declare another to stand in his place."

"Has this ever happened before?"

"Not in my lifetime. Erdogan has ruled for as long as I have existed, and nobody has been strong enough to oppose him."

"But you think we can?"

"I believe Colonel Taylor can, with help."

"Well, think you can do it?" White asked of Taylor.

"If the survival of us all depends upon it, I will find a way," he replied confidently.

Deep down he knew what a monumental threat Erdogan presented, but he could not admit it, or they could never embark on their mission.

"Then it is decided!" Lasure said, "At 1800 hours the fleet will depart for Earth, and we will not come back. We either take our homes back, or we die trying."

He quickly turned and left, but White remained at Taylor's side.

"You know what you've just gotten us into?"

"The most dangerous and best chance we ever had of winning this war."

"I sure hope you're right."

Silva stepped forward and snatched the drink from Taylor's hands.

"You've got four hours, Colonel. Get some rest. We need you on top form."

Taylor was appalled at his tone, yet accepted it was true. He stumbled over to his quarters and collapsed into bed just seconds after stripping off his armour. It seemed like no time at all had passed when he felt something tugging on his shirt and awoke to find Silva once more standing over him.

"Is it time already?" he croaked.

Silva smiled. "Afraid so."

Taylor pulled on his armour and stepped outside to see

a very different sight to when he had gone to rest. All but three of the human ships had lifted off, the three that were too badly damaged to take to the skies.

"Irala find us our targets?"

"He sure came through."

Taylor then watched dozens of small transport craft lift off from the surface. He looked out across to the bar that had accommodated so many thousands of their people. It was dead now. Everything had been left behind.

"You know I'm gonna miss this place, Sergeant."

"Really?"

"Find a place where you can rest easy at night and not wake up to find some bastard trying to blow your head off, that's a lot to like."

"I have had Charlie Company assemble aboard the Baron. Admiral Lasure has requested that we accompany him personally."

Taylor nodded in response. He knelt down and pressed his hand into the sand until he felt rock beneath. He gripped a pile of the sand and let it pass out of his hand.

"This could be the last time we ever see this place," he whispered, "It has done us a damn good turn, as has its inhabitants."

"All things must come to an end, Colonel."

"Don't say that. Certainly don't repeat it. We've been fighting to prove otherwise all this time."

"We should go, Sir."

Taylor stood back up and followed him to the copter awaiting them. It was one of the last human transports still on the surface. He climbed aboard to find just Jafar and Lang aboard, as well as Rains at the helm.

"We're going home! And this time it's for good! Woohoo!" yelled Rains. They shut the door, and he powered up the engines.

"Didn't think I'd ever regret leaving this place," said Taylor.

"It is the resting place of Eli, so it was always going to be difficult to leave. But you can come back when this is all over and take her home."

Taylor shook his head.

"No, she's been laid to rest, and I shall not trouble her any further."

They were soon breaking out into orbit where the fleet awaited them. They could see the civilian barges had already separated, and a number of Aranui vessels remained in position around them. Taylor soon found himself strolling on the bridge of the Diderot where Lasure awaited him alongside White and Irala. Much of the bridge had been hastily repaired following the previous engagement.

"Welcome aboard, Taylor," said Lasure.

"Are you sure you want to go through with this now? Should this fail, we will not get another chance," said White.

"I've never been more sure of anything in my life,

General. All roads have led to this day. When we left Earth, we were a weak and defeated people. But now it is us who choose the time and place that we fight. Their forces are divided, and it is us who have the element of surprise."

"We still don't have the numbers to win in an all out war," said White, "Not even close."

"We don't have to. We aren't in this for the long fight. All we need do is cause chaos and draw him out."

"Taylor, I have taken the liberty of selecting targets from a list Irala has compiled for us. We will hit twenty targets. Twelve of which are in Europe where we presume Erdogan is most likely to be. Other targets across the world will ensure we have a presence on every continent, but we will be spread thin in most locations. There are only so many of us."

"Good. Our opening attacks should strike them hard and remove their capacity to retaliate quickly. I want utter chaos. I want to strike fear into our enemy. We'll hit them so hard in the first wave that they will dread the second."

"A second assault that will never come," White added.

"But they don't know that."

"Our attacks on the ground forces, industry, and aircraft on Earth were more successful than you might have imagined," Irala said, "If we are quick to despatch the fleet in orbit, we will have supremacy of the skies."

"Almost makes you wonder why we ever left Earth," said Taylor, "but we were never this strong. We were never this focused, and only through the help of Irala and his people have we made it this far. Can you believe it? For all the hatred we had of aliens, and yet we needed aliens to save us and give us this opportunity to come back? Will you come with me? Will you fight with us?" he asked Irala.

"I will remain aboard the Diderot and man a Guardian. I will be at your side throughout."

"And when that is destroyed?"

Then I shall take up another. I can be both by your side and here to advise and assist your Admiral."

"So, General, I assume you have selected a target for my Regiment?" Taylor asked.

"Warsaw," he quickly replied, "It is home to one of the greatest troops in Erdogan's army. They are called the Sampions."

Taylor had never heard the name.

"Warriors from my world, and two others like it," said Jafar.

"As many as a thousand of them reside in the city itself, with many thousands of Mech warriors supporting them."

"Reside?"

"They have made it their home, Colonel," added White, "For most of the Krys the war has been over for some time."

"And the human populace?"

"Some fled to Ony with us, others were captured and now work as slaves. Many more we don't know about.

Thousands still work in the city itself, serving their Krys masters."

"We're ready to jump when you are," said Lasure.

"Not exactly going into this with a lot of planning?"

"Just your sort of style I thought," replied White, "I have already had detailed maps of the area sent to your Mappad, as well as a full list of everyone going in with you. You'll have close to five thousand troops to take the city."

"So probably the same as they have? And you tell me they're the elite?"

"Yes, but you'll be striking with the element of surprise. I thought this would be good odds for you?"

Taylor almost smiled.

"We'll make it work."

"Colonel, I want you en route to your destination within three minutes of our arrival. There is no time to waste. In these few short hours we have put more into this operation than I think you can imagine."

"I understand, Admiral."

He turned to leave for his craft.

"Colonel, before you go, I have someone who wants to see you."

He turned and was surprised to see the door to the Admiral's quarters open, and Coco stepped out. Taylor strode quickly towards her and stopped dead in front of where she stood.

"You shouldn't be here," he pleaded.

"She'll be safe here," added Lasure, "She'll have the finest of medical attention and will be as safe as she can be."

"You still shouldn't have come."

"You have already said that if this fails, it is over. I am putting my faith in you, Mitch."

It was the first time he had been called that by any woman since Eli, and it silenced him completely.

"You can do this, Mitch. You were born to do it. Every day of your life has led you to this. You can win," she said.

She reached forward and kissed him. He froze and didn't know how to react. She pulled back and smiled as tears slid down her face.

"We'll be waiting for you, both of us."

He couldn't bring himself to respond or make promises he couldn't keep. He ran his hand down her cheek and brushed some of the tears away, and finally carried on past her without a single word. He knew there was nothing he could say. More than anything it was a reminder of the friends he had lost, and allies he could well do with now. He stopped at the exit to the bridge and looked back to Lasure and White one last time.

"This is it. There is no retreat. There are no more chances. We do not hesitate, we do not stop, and we do not falter, or we lose. There is no room for weakness or sentiment. We are in this to the very end, victory or death."

"We're with you," said White.

"Initiate jump when ready."

He turned and left with Jafar by his side.

"You think I got the message across?" Taylor asked him as they strode towards the docking bays.

"Yes."

"And you?"

"I am ready."

"For what?"

"Anything."

Taylor couldn't argue with that.

"I am surprised they did not insist you stay behind. You are, after all, more important than I am if this works. How did you swing it?"

"I told them I go where you go, and if I am not at the final fight of this war, I will never be accepted as their leader."

"Fair enough."

They climbed aboard Rains' ship and wondered if it would be the last time. Before he could say a word, the Admiral's voice came over an open comms channel.

"This is Admiral Lasure. You all know what you have to do. This is the greatest and probably last opportunity we will ever have to secure the existence of the human race. Stick to the plan, and see this through. And remember, we have Taylor and his Immortals at the spearhead of this operation. Remember their victories, and go forth to pursue such greatness of your own. Good luck to you all."

"Well that was short," Rains laughed.

"What more do you say to a race of people on their last legs about to throw down for one last try?" Silva asked.

"I guess I'd try and be a little more upbeat about it," he jested with a smile that caused Silva to jab him in the shoulder.

"This really the end?" Morris asked of Taylor.

"Beginning of it, one way or another," he replied sternly.

"What makes you so sure?"

"My gut."

"All vessels prepare to jump in five minutes," said a voice over the comms.

Taylor leaned over Rains' seat to whisper in his ear.

"All bullshit aside. You've been one hell of a pilot. Were it not for you, we would have been dead a long time ago. Just see us through to the end, you hear?"

"You think I plan on dying after all this? I have put in way too much work to see it all end now."

"Seriously, you've been a great pilot, a great fighter, and a great friend. My friends don't seem all that lucky. I wish you to see this one to the end and live to tell the tale."

He nodded in gratitude but couldn't keep a straight face more than a few seconds.

"As will you. You're the great Colonel Taylor. You can't die."

"We can all die," he replied softly, "I might be a little harder to kill than the average, but time catches us all."

"Then let it be a glorious death when it comes," said Rains. He reached up and patted Taylor on the shoulder.

He was never capable of being serious for even a minute, but Taylor knew that was his coping mechanism, and he wouldn't rob him of it.

"You know if you make it through this, they'll probably build a statue of you bigger than the Statue of Liberty herself. Hell, they might even put it where she stood. Don't think there's much left of her now."

"And if I fail, Eddie, I'll vanish into obscurity."

"Not a chance. Win or lose, you've more than left your mark in this world. Lose and you'll forever be remembered as the biggest pain in the ass to the Krys race."

"Nothing ever gets you down, does it, Eddie?"

"Way I figure it, when you're staring in the face of the annihilation of your entire race, you can either laugh or cry."

"Yeah, but you've always been like this, so what was your excuse before the invasion?"

"Hell, you got me," he replied with a smile.

Taylor sat down and looked over the data on his Mappad. It was alarming how little information they actually had. He looked back up to the platoon inside the copter. They all watched him and eagerly awaited some words of encouragement.

"You all know the plan?"

"Yes, Sir!" they shouted in unison.

"We go in, and we kill all that we can. There aren't any egos to contend with here. You get a shot at Erdogan; you take it. Just remember that this is the big one. Everything we have done up to this day counts for nothing unless we can succeed here. It's a big task, but nothing we haven't faced before. The enemy will be unsuspecting and ill prepared for our attack. You press that advantage at every stage. Shock and awe, people!"

"One minute to jump."

"Okay, not long now. Get ready for the ride of your life," said Eddie.

Taylor shook his head. He couldn't work out who the statement was for, until he realised it was Rains merely psyching himself up.

"Jafar, these Sampions?"

"What of them?"

"They good?"

"Yes."

"How come we haven't come across them before?"

"You have, just in small numbers where they counted for little. They lead Mech forces; act as bodyguards, and in extreme cases, elite shock troops. They were never needed for that purpose in this last war. When in numbers, they are a formidable force."

"Well how many more are there like them?"

"Probably not more than a few thousand on Earth."

"Why so many in Warsaw, then?"

"Class structure. They live among their equals."

"So what? We just drew the short straw and are hitting the hardest mother fuckers Erdogan has to offer?"

"General White specified targets based on the ability of those units selected for the task."

"Once again, we do good, and we get rewarded with a kick in the ass for it," replied Taylor, but he was smiling now.

"That's okay," said Silva, "If they're like you, they shouldn't be any trouble at all," he said to Jafar.

The alien did not get the joke, but Silva still laughed at it himself and was joined by several others.

"You would be wise to not underestimate the Sampions. They are brave and capable warriors."

"Jump in ten, nine, eight…"

"Here we go boys!" yelled Rains.

"Seven, six, five, four…"

"We're going home!"

"Three, two, one…jump."

It took a few moments for them to pass through the gateway, and they felt the gravity shift as they always had done. Taylor was quick on his feet once they were on the far side and was looking intently and scanning from one of Rains' screens to another. The scanner began to bleep as it recorded activity.

"There they are," stated Rains.

Taylor was counting the numbers on the screen before them.

"Thirty warships and about the right amount of support vessels and fighters. Must be most of what they got left here," said Rains.

Lights flashed from the long range guns of the Diderot springing to life, and Taylor realised they had jumped straight into range with the enemy fleet. He knew that was no accident.

"Admiral ain't wasting no time," said Rains.

The docking bay doors opened soon after, and they could see dozens of allied warships approach the enemy fleet and screen them off for a path down to Earth. They were welcomed by a beautiful view of the Earth down below. Cloud cover was minimal, and they were looking down into the centre of the Pacific and could just make out the coastlines that skirted either side.

"Beautiful, ain't it, Colonel?"

"Always, Eddie. It's what we fight for. Don't let this be the last time we see it."

"Ye of so little faith."

He reached forward and put all power to the engines, and they raced out of the docking bay and out into space. Pulses flashed past their position, and Taylor watched the screens as the battle ensued at their flank. He could see the enemy vessels being bombarded with far more than they were putting out.

"Good luck to them."

He turned his attention to what was ahead. They were at the very front of the assault. The screens showing their flanks revealed hundreds of copters with them and many hundreds more vessels far larger. Rains pointed up to the screen above him that was the rear display screen, and Taylor looked up and found he was speechless. Thousands of vessels were at their back. It was the largest operation he had seen since their departure from Earth. The sensation was like a high, and in that moment, he felt immortal.

CHAPTER ELEVEN

They had passed through the atmosphere in no time at all and with no losses they could see. They were coming in just over Northern Italy and descending quickly. Taylor expected to see anti aircraft fire at any time, but it never came.

"Right on target, right on schedule," Rains commented proudly. "Warsaw, hey? Always wanted to go there," he added.

"Few years ago, maybe, but I don't think you'll find it quite so welcoming today," replied Taylor.

Missile trails rushed out ahead of them as the larger vessels in the assault began to bombard ground targets while they made their approach. The city looked untouched by the wars that had plagued the world for so many years.

"Not putting up much of a fight are they?" Rains asked.

"Give it time."

They were descending quickly towards the city, and they could make out the movement of both humans and aliens below. A few pulses from small arms flew past, and the armour of their craft brushed two aside. Rains manoeuvred them in between several buildings and past the first enemy.

"Thirty seconds," he said.

Taylor turned back to the platoon.

"If they're alien, you shoot them. Humans are considered non-combatants unless they declare themselves otherwise."

"What about clones?" Silva asked.

"We won't know what's what until they start taking shots at us. I will not risk killing civilians until we know for sure."

He reached over and hit the door release buttons so that the exits opened up either side of the fuselage. Rains lifted the nose and brought them to an abrupt hover twenty metres above the ground on one of the main streets of the city.

"Go!" Taylor hollered as he was jumping out of one of the doors.

He hit the ground running and rushed to the cover of the entrance hallway of a department store at the side of the street. He expected to take fire any second, but nothing came. He watched as the last of his unit dropped in, and Rains broke for the skies.

"Good luck, Colonel!" he said over the comms.

Taylor looked around in all directions and expected to be fired upon any second.

"Where the hell is everyone?" Silva shouted.

Taylor looked around to see that his platoon and the two that had jumped in after them had taken up defensive positions. They were so used to having to hunker down for cover that none of them thought to carry onwards.

"We have to move on. We can't let them organise," said Taylor.

He got up and gestured for the others to follow him. He clung close to the buildings on one side of the street and could see Matthews' platoon mirroring their movements on the far side. He came to an abrupt halt when he reached a cafeteria and was astonished to find three human staff members standing frozen behind the counter.

"Go!" he yelled to them instinctively, but he soon realised there was no logic in his order, as he knew they had nowhere to go. He nudged the door open a little.

"What are you still doing here?"

"Have you come to rescue us?" one of the men asked.

Taylor shook his head. "We're here to seek out and kill alien forces in the area."

"Then we will take our chances."

Hew shook his head but could see that they had accepted their fate, and he himself could not promise them anything better.

"Come on," whispered Silva from outside.

He obliged and carried on along the street. It was eerily silent for a town they knew was inhabited, or occupied depending on your point of view. A high-pitched scream came from one of the side streets as they came up along side it. It was a battle cry, and several Krys rushed at them with guns blazing. Taylor ducked down. The bottom edge of his shield hit the road, and he was covered from head to toe as he opened fire. There were just five aliens coming at them. They looked much like Jafar did when he was not wearing armour. Each of them was firing a handheld pulse weapon that seemed to be fitted into their forearms, and they all carried a curved blade in the other hand that was almost a metre long.

Reitech rounds punctured the first two multiple times and met little resistance, but the third and fourth creatures were only clipped lightly as they rushed the troops of the Inter-Allied. Silva collapsed under the weight of one of the wounded creatures and was still firing on full auto into its torso as it collapsed and crushed him flat beneath his shield. The other wounded Mech went after Jafar while the last of them rushed Taylor. Several shots from the creature's gun struck the barrel of his and caused it to snap out of his hands.

Taylor had just enough time to draw his Assegai as the creature smashed into his shield with what almost felt like the force of a juggernaut. He was thrown back a few paces, but the creature stuck with him so that his comrades could not fire in his aid. The creature swung at him with its blade, but it was not the clumsy strike of a Mech, but a calculated and controlled one just as Jafar would deliver. Taylor ducked down and raised his shield as the blade connected. Sparks flew, and the blade seemed to light up with electricity and cut almost ten centimetres into the rim of his shield.

He pushed off with his shield and thrust up with his Assegai as he drew it from its sheath. He fully expected to drive it deep into his attacker's stomach, but the alien turned and yanked the edge of his shield so that he was spun around. The blade came at him once again, and he narrowly ducked under and smashed the edge of his shield up into its torso. As the alien was launched off its feet, it fired its arm-mounted weapon at him. He raised his shield in time, and the shots bounced off the thick armour, giving his people the opening they needed. Silva and two others of his platoon opened fire with multiple bursts into the creature until it dropped dead to the pavement.

Taylor scrambled back up onto his feet and looked down at the body of the creature.

"Getting slow in your old age, Colonel," Silva joked.

"That a Sampion?" Taylor asked.

"Yes," replied Jafar confidently.

"They came at us with some kind of frenzy, but they must have known they would die?"

"Yes," Jafar replied again.

"So they really are as good as you say?" Taylor said to Jafar rhetorically, "They had no armour, and only the weapons they had to hand. They would have been a handful if they'd been ready for this."

"They are the best of the Krys people."

"You regret their loss Jafar?" Silva asked.

He nodded. "They are fine warriors."

A single pulse smashed into the building next to them, and they turned to see a dozen Mechs advancing down the street towards them. Taylor smiled as he felt a familiarity that put him in his comfort zone. For a brief moment he thought back to the Moon when he had first encountered a Mech warrior and how terrifying they were, and then smiled again at how humble they now seemed compared to his own people. But before he could react, Irala's Guardian stormed between their lines and went right for the Mechs.

It was firing from both of its weapons, and the Mech warriors were just not fast enough to avoid its wrath. Taylor rushed on towards them with his Assegai still in hand. The Guardian soaked up all the fire, and he advanced without incident and was able to rush at one of the creatures as it frantically tried to defend itself against the Guardian that was cutting its comrades apart, and even stamped on one on the way.

Taylor drove his Assegai deep. The creature turned,

and he smashed his shield into its pulse cannon so that it was stopped dead. Disabled and helpless, the creature let go of its weapon and reached for Taylor, but he thrust his Assegai down the centreline. It passed though the creature's armour and ran up to the hilt. Its hands tried to get a grip against his helmet, but the life was already seeping out from the creature. Taylor drew out his blade and ran on; the Mech dropped dead to the road.

Looking around the street, he could see the Mech force that had approached them was now reduced to a heap of twisted metal and bodies. He looked up at more craft passing overhead and their own people leaping out and descending onto roofs and into the streets around them.

"Feels good, doesn't it?" asked Silva, "To be hitting them where it hurts."

Taylor nodded. "Let's move on."

They carried on into the next street and found a car haring down the street towards them. Taylor and his people clung to the sidewalks. Two humans were inside the vehicle, and they looked terrified.

"What are they running from?" asked Morris, "Us, the Krys? Both?"

"Everything," replied Taylor, "They just want to live."

They could hear gunfire in the distance, and it was a reminder for them to keep going. Taylor led the way and took a bend up ahead. A Mech ran past, totally oblivious to him. He took aim and fired three shots that killed the creature instantly. Even before it had fallen down dead, another six appeared before him. But they weren't heading for Taylor. They were passing from one side of the road to another. They were running from allied troops.

"Take them down!" Taylor ordered.

As he opened fire, another dozen ran into view, and not one of them tried to return fire. They were running in fear for their lives. The whole of Taylor's platoon was lined up like a shooting range now. Dozens more rushed into view, and Taylor had to slam in a new magazine to keep firing.

"Damn turkey shoot!" Silva shouted with glee.

They kept up the fire relentlessly and cut down dozens of the Mechs. Only a few got past them, and several from the platoon shouted out with excitement at their luck. Taylor felt no remorse for them at all, but neither did he take any pleasure in it. As the last of them were finished off, he carried on around the bend to pursue the rest. As he took the bend, he found a hail of pulses smash into the ground ahead, and one struck his shield. He leapt back around the corner as another pulse soared past him.

He peered around the corner very carefully. He could just see a narrow slit in the ground floor of a building up ahead. He turned back to Silva and Jafar who were waiting close by his side.

"Fortified bunker built into the ground level just as we saw before," he said.

"That ain't so bad," replied Silva. "Can we go around

it?"

"No time. We jump it."

"Like you did before? That's crazy. Okay you got away with it once, but that was then."

"Yeah and this is now. I want three volunteers."

Silva shook his head, and yet he said, "I'm in," at the same time. Jafar nodded also. Herrera had been listening in.

"Count me in."

"You all know what to do," said Taylor, pulling a grenade from his armour.

"Three, two, one…"

He rushed out from cover. Lights flashed ahead almost instantly, but he quickly jumped and used his boosters to leap several storeys up, coming down in front of the bunker and below the gun loop. He armed the grenade, and the others did the same before throwing them in and ducking for cover.

Explosions rang out as a hole was blasted in the front of the bunker, and Taylor put his rifle through and opened fire. He cut down the remaining two Mechs, not giving them time to recover, but none of them were Sampions.

"Taylor, come in!" King called over the comms.

The sound of gunfire raged in the background.

"What can I do for you, Captain?" Taylor asked. The dust was still settling on his armour.

"We're two klicks north of your position. We're trying

to enter the artificial garden complex there, but we're meeting heavy resistance."

"Artificial garden? What the fuck is that?"

"It's what it says on the billboards, Colonel. A good few hundred of the enemy have retreated inside, your Sampions. It's a massive dome complex, so you can't miss it. There are only a few entrances in or out. We're at the southern entrance. All other exits have been closed off by other units."

Taylor rubbed his chin as he tried to fathom out what he was hearing.

"Why would they have gone in there, Jafar? There's no chance of escape, so why?"

"To die a good death," Jafar quickly replied.

"Then I guess we'll just have to oblige them. We'll be with you shortly, Captain," he replied down the comms and gestured for the three platoons at his back to follow on. They passed through several empty streets before eventually catching sight of the massive domed complex at the end of a long road ahead.

"All the nature on Earth and some stupid idiot built an artificial garden, inside and away from the elements?" Taylor asked of Silva.

"Doesn't make any sense to me either. Guess some people just don't like getting a little wet and dirty, Colonel."

"It's what we've been fighting for, isn't it? All that this world has to offer us? We take this world back, and I'll be sure to have that shit levelled."

"Why wait? Looks like we've got the perfect opportunity," Silva said, smiling.

Taylor lifted up his Mappad to check the progress of their assault being reported live sector by sector. He couldn't believe what a relief it was to have access to their communications and not be jammed like they had through so much of the war.

"Doesn't look like much of the city has put up a fight."

"We hit 'em hard, so they didn't have time to get organised."

"These Sampions, all they want is a good death?" Taylor asked Jafar.

"Or to live to fight another day. They are not stupid."

Taylor was surprised to hear his response.

"They are like you?"

"In some ways."

Five Mechs appeared at an opening to their right flank, and an unarmoured Sampion led them. Jafar noticed them first and opened fire without hesitation. The Sampion ducked back down for the cover of a flatbed truck, and four of the Mechs followed suit; the fifth struck by a volley of fire. Taylor could see what Jafar meant by the Sampions now. They led like officers and NCOs.

Taylor twisted the primer on one of his grenades and tossed it along the road so that it slid underneath the truck and came out amongst the Mechs. Before it ignited, he ran and leapt up into the air. As the explosion rang out, he landed on the cab of the truck and opened fire on full auto. Two of the Mechs were killed by the blast, and a third was badly wounded. Taylor's fire put that one out of its misery. He then turned his attention on the Sampion. The creature rolled out of his line of fire, and his magazine ran dry as he tried to follow his target.

Without hesitation, Taylor leapt towards the creature and landed on it with his shield held firmly before him. He smashed the alien to the ground, rolling over it, and landed back on his feet. He pulled out his Assegai. The creature turned to face him, but before they could fight, several shots rang out. Silva had strafed the creature in the back, and it dropped down dead.

Taylor felt robbed of the kill, but more than that, he felt shame that the creature had not gotten the honourable death he seemed to feel it deserved.

"You okay, Colonel?" Silva asked. He stood frozen and looking as the corpse of the Sampion. The creature could just as well have been his friend Jafar, and even Tsengal. Finally, he snapped out of it and turned to carry on their journey, but he could not put the thought of the Sampion out of his head.

As they closed the distance to the domed complex ahead, they could see King directing Italian troops that had come to their assistance. They were stuck at the entrance to the complex where a bitter battle was raging. Cars and trucks had been turned over and formed a barricade around the entrance that the allies were using for cover, and pulses rushed out from the entrance. It already looked like a siege that had been raging for hours or possibly days. King turned and sighed in relief on seeing Taylor arrival.

"Looks like you've got a bit of a battle on your hands, Captain," said Taylor.

"They're dug in something fierce."

"We could call in a strike? Flatten the whole complex?"

Taylor shook his head at Silva. "And if they were protecting Erdogan in there? We'd never get the answer we need."

"He ain't in there, Colonel," King added.

"And you know that for sure? You're willing to bet all our lives on it? You know we have to kill that bastard Erdogan, and we have to be seen killing him, and in an honourable fashion, too. Then we have to present his body. No, we take this building and kill all who are inside."

"We can't go through every single alien until we find him, you know?"

Taylor glared at King and refused to give a verbal answer.

"You got it," he finally replied as he gave in.

"We can't get in through the entrances," said Taylor, "so let's open this monstrosity up like the tin can it is, and go in through the roof."

He lifted his Mappad and selected the rooftops as a

target by punching in his access codes. He looked back to Silva.

"We're going up and over, so should be another turkey shoot when we get up there. Be ready."

They waited a few minutes as the battle continued to rage on at the southern entrance. Then they saw several missile trails come out of the clouds above and head towards the building. They struck the rooftop with such an immense impact that they felt the ground beneath them rumble. Metal debris and shrapnel was thrown out over them and across the road. Taylor stood up slowly and saw that a fifty-metre wide hole had been blasted out of the cap of the dome.

"Let's go!" he yelled.

He ran out from cover as pulses from the ground entrance forces fired on them, but he was in the air in seconds. The vast domed complex had such a shallow incline that he landed twenty metres up and immediately started running up the roof and to the breach. It took a minute to reach the damaged area. The rooftop beneath his feet was as solid as the deck of a ship. He quickly reached the crest and looked in at the most amazing tropical gardens he could ever have imagined. It was a bizarre and surreal sight, but he was soon brought back to reality when several pulses flashed past his head.

Taylor took aim at the creatures below and opened fire. There were so many of them that they were like cattle herded together. Some tried to spread out and take cover amongst the trees and bushes inside, but it did little to save them. Taylor had emptied an entire magazine and was loading in another when he looked around him. Sixty of his own people were unloading into the breach and cutting down the Sampions below with little effort at all.

Many returned fire, but their small arms came to little effect at the troops of the Inter-Allied firing on them from the cover of the rooftop. He thought back to the one Silva had shot in the back, and then further back into his past when he first met Jafar and Tsengal. He remembered the massive leap of faith that was required from both parties, and he began to weep.

"Stop firing!" he screamed, "Hold your fire!" He lifted up his comms unit and yelled once again, "Hold you fire!"

The troops quickly obliged without question, but they still looked to him surprise and confused. The area all around them was completely silenced. Not a single Reitech rifle fired, and the Sampions below recognised the respite for what it was and made no attempt to return fire.

"What are you doing, Colonel?" Morris asked in amazement, "We have a chance to end them now. The best and most elite soldiers Erdogan has, and they're like fish in a barrel."

"And if it was us down there? What would you want to happen here?"

"I've been down there. I've stood where they are now,

and I've watched my friends die. Let's end them now while we have the chance!" Morris pleaded.

He leaned in over the edge and tried to take aim with his rifle, but Taylor took hold of his shoulder and wrenched him back from the edge.

"You'll do as you're ordered, Captain," Taylor stated sternly.

Everyone looked to Taylor for the next move, including the enemy who peered up from the gardens below. Taylor stepped over to Jafar to talk privately. Most of the others on the rooftop looked at each other in amazement. Others looked in on the enemy with suspicion.

"You told me these Sampions are something special, like you?"

Jafar nodded.

"You came over to our cause, so why not them?"

"I do not believe it possible."

"Why not? What makes you so special that you fight with us and they won't?"

Jafar shrugged. The Guardian strode up onto the rooftop to join them, stopping as Irala's projection appeared before it.

"Taylor, you cannot reason with these animals," Irala said firmly.

But he looked to Jafar and shook his head.

"I stand beside one of them now, and another alien. I have learnt to trust you both and call you friends. I refuse to believe you are the only ones."

Jafar seemed to have mixed feelings and chose not to comment.

"They cannot be trusted," added Irala.

"I guess that's about what they think of us," replied Taylor.

He turned his back on Irala and strode to the edge of the crater in the roof and stood in plain view of the enemy below. He could see dozens of them, maybe even a hundred. He unclipped his rifle in full view of them all and threw it aside. His shield soon followed it, and he now stood at the edge empty handed.

"This is not a sensible course of action."

But Taylor totally ignored Irala's comment. He leapt into the breach and descended with his boosters. The Sampions parted as he made his descent and landed in a clearing they had created. They formed a circle around him twenty-metres wide, and not one of them made an attempt to close that distance. They seemed in awe of his tenacity and strength before them. He turned and turned and studied them all. None of them were armoured, and they were equipped with just small arms and a few pulse cannons they had salvaged from the Mechs.

Deep down Taylor was terrified. He knew they could tear him apart at will if they desired, but he stood tall and proud and didn't dare show an ounce of fear.

"I am Colonel Mitch Taylor of the Inter-Allied

Regiment!" he roared.

It was clear to him that they did not recognise his face, but the name meant everything, and yet still none of them moved or said a word. So he went on, although he was making it up as he went along, as he'd never given any thought of being in such a situation.

"You don't have to keep living under the control of Erdogan!" he shouted, "You're the greatest of your people, and what do you get for that? Fight for me, and I'll set you free."

He could not tell if they were unimpressed or considering the offer; their expressions barely changed.

"Tell me Erdogan is a fair and good leader? You deserve better than that, and I am offering that to you!"

He pointed up to Jafar who stood in full view at the edge of the collapsed roof above them.

"Jafar saw his chance to get away from the shackles of your Lords, and now he stands beside us as an equal! Join me!"

Finally, one of the aliens stepped into the circle, and all of them looked to him. It was clear he held rank over them. He took several paces forward and stopped just two metres from Taylor.

"Well?" he asked the alien.

"I am Sarik," stated the alien, "Second Captain to Erdogan's private guard."

Taylor was impressed and realised he was talking to the

right alien.

"Tell me, Sarik, has Erdogan been a fair commander to you?"

"He has gotten us this place on Earth, the paradise."

"And when I kill Erdogan, what will you do, then?"

The alien was silenced.

"I will end this war, and I will kill Erdogan, just like I have killed all who have stood before me. Join us now, and ensure there is a future for you in this paradise."

The creature thought on it for just a few seconds and then gave his reply.

"We will only follow a strong leader. If you can defeat me in single combat, you will have our allegiance. No weapons, no armour. We fight in the old way."

Taylor wanted to gasp at the prospect. He looked at the towering alien, but he held his breath and knew it was worth the risk.

"Agreed!" he shouted for all to hear.

Silva and Morris shook this heads in disbelief, but Jafar only looked in out of curiosity and respect for Taylor's bravery. Sarik grinned at the prospect and put down the blade he was carrying. Taylor took off his helmet and unclipped the harnesses of his suit and stepped out. The alien unclipped its arm mounted pulse weapon.

Taylor stood before the creature in just his BDU now, with nothing more than his own hands and feet to defend him. He felt naked to the world, and being so weak when surrounded by the Krys was terrifying. He tried to put it out of his mind and focus on the creature. Sarik wore a body-fitting suit that appeared to provide no more protection than the camouflage BDU Taylor was wearing. The alien stood half a metre taller than he did.

Sarik began to circle the opening amongst his warriors that had become their arena. Taylor could already tell from the way he moved that he was an experienced and well-trained fighter.

What the hell have I got myself into? Taylor asked himself.

He remembered when he first fought in hand-to-hand combat with a wounded Mech warrior in France, and it was a terrifying experience then. Despite all of his experience, this was every bit as frightening as that had been. Sarik led with his hands high and palms down like a Thai boxer. He suddenly jabbed forward with a quick snap with his left that struck Taylor's jaw and caused him to recoil back.

The impact was so hard he felt it in his neck, but he had barely seen it coming. He stumbled two paces back before regaining his footing. Just as he had recovered, the creature came at him again with a powerful hammer blow. Taylor raised his left arm to parry, but the power was too much. The impact drove through and struck him in the head and forced him down onto one knee. While he was still stunned, he felt the creature's knee drive into his chest, and he was flattened to the ground.

Taylor coughed and tried to get to his feet, finding

blood on his hand as he cupped his mouth. He thought back to the training sessions he had with Jafar, and wondered if his friend had gone too easy on him. He got to his feet and immediately found Sarik bearing down on him again. The creature delivered four straight punches in quick succession. The first he stopped, the second drove into his stomach, the third he just managed to dodge, but the fourth struck his stomach again, and he felt the wind come out of him.

He collapsed back into a seated position. Sarik appeared to wait for him to stand. It was clear that for anything he might have been, the creature was at least sporting.

"You're good," Taylor said, blood dripping from his mouth, and he began to smile.

He knew he couldn't beat Sarik in a stand up fight, and all of the equipment and technology he had gotten accustomed to wearing had given him a false sense of security in that regard. He shook his head to wake himself up, and knew now that he had to take a different approach.

Sarik came at him again with a powerful push kick. This time he didn't try and take the force of the blow. He leapt aside and punched forward into the creature's flank. The impact hurt Sarik, and he folded slightly and brought his head down to Taylor's level; an opportunity he was quick to take. Taylor swung with all his force and connected with the creature's flat nose. It was like hitting iron. Pain soared through his arm, but the creature staggered back a few paces before regaining its balance.

Taylor's confidence was back now as he approached the alien. Sarik lashed out at him with a quick jab. He ducked under and drove an uppercut into the towering creatures' stomach, but as he rose up to strike again, the alien retorted with a head butt, following it with an elbow that knocked Taylor onto the flat of his back. A stamp attack came next, and he rolled out and onto his feet just in time.

Taylor had just a few seconds to catch his breath before the alien came at him again. He spun out from one of its strikes and tried to back fist Sarik in the head, but the creature pre-empted him and moved in, locking him in a bear hug. His was an iron grip, and Taylor struggled to get free. He could feel the energy being sapped away from him as he tried to fight the grip. He looked down at the huge feet of the creature either side of his. He raised his right foot and drove his heel down with all his force onto Sarik's foot that seemed to be covered with nothing more than the fabric of his suit. Sarik let out a groan in pain.

Taylor seized his opportunity as he felt the creature's grip weaken. He took hold of one of the fingers on Sarik's left hand that held him in a vice grip. With a firm grip around the creature's finger, he snapped it back so that the finger broke. The creature's grip was broken, and he pushed out and away. He watched in amazement as Sarik took hold of his crooked broken finger and snapped it back into position without showing any pain at all.

Sarik stormed forwards and threw a straight punch. Taylor avoided it but landed in a standing bind. Sarik drove his knee up so high it struck Taylor's chin. The impact snapped his head back and almost knocked him out, and he knew he couldn't take another like it. He dropped down and took hold of Sarik's legs and pulled them out from under him. The back of the alien's head landed hard against a rock and stunned him. It was the chance Taylor needed. He dropped down onto the alien and drove punch after punch into his face.

Just when he thought he'd won, the alien threw a wild hook that knocked him sideways, and he rolled over and finally climbed back onto his feet. Sarik was back up now also, but he was looking weary and weak. Taylor took a deep breath and approached fearlessly. Sarik threw a heavy strike towards his head, but Taylor ducked under and around and leapt onto his back in one swift manoeuvre. He had the alien in a chokehold now, and he held on for dear life.

Sarik reached around and struck him, but the hits were weak compared to what Taylor had been dealt earlier in the fight. Finally, the alien dropped to its knees and lost its strength. He let his grip go just before the alien passed out, took a step around, and dealt a crushing hook into Sarik's face. The force of the impact almost broke Taylor's hand, but Sarik collapsed onto his side with blood seeping out from his mouth and nose. He was gasping for air and painfully lifted his hand up to ask for Taylor to stop.

Taylor staggered back a few steps and could feel his knees were weak. His ribs hurt like they were bruised or broken and his face numb from the impacts. He took a few paces forward and loomed over the defeated alien.

"Do you submit?"

Sarik looked up and nodded. He showed no shame or disappointment in his defeat. Taylor extended his hand to Sarik and helped him to his feet.

"So?"

"If we follow you, then it is until Erdogan is dead, or we are."

"That's the plan," said Taylor.

"Then yes. You have my word, and that of all here. We will follow you."

Taylor nodded in appreciation before looking up to see the disgruntled and worried faces of Jafar and Irala still watching in overhead.

CHAPTER TWELVE

"You can't trust them, Colonel."

Taylor looked up to see Irala standing over him. He was sitting and resting from his wounds, trying to get a little peace. He turned away and watched Sarik and many of his Sampions step out from an armoury building. They were now fully armoured and equipped, and more of them flooded in there to do the same.

"You of all people should know the dangers of having such a formidable number of the enemy among us can be," added Irala.

Taylor noted that Jafar was standing over him also.

"Not you, too?"

"Irala is right. I know you think Sarik and his force can aid us, but they may just as well try to kill us."

"You tried to kill me when we first met," Taylor said accusingly, "and so did you," he added, staring at Irala.

273

Neither of them looked convinced.

"You're just gonna both have to take a leap of faith, just like I have."

"And if that leap takes us to our deaths?"

"Then it won't matter, Irala, because then you won't have anything left to worry about."

It didn't convince either of them, but he found it almost funny. Sarik strode over to them. He was even more intimidating now that he wore his armour. It was the close fitting and intricately designed suits reserved only for the finest of Krys warriors. His armour was a satin black with just a little shimmer.

"You can't keep that look, you know. You'll be shot at by every man and woman in our armies."

Sarik nodded. He raised his left forearm and pressed a few buttons on the control pad. His armour faded to white, and the others soon followed suit. It was an amazing sight, and Taylor was speechless.

"We fight for the white man, so we wear white in your honour."

"Not all white!" Silva shouted in response.

Taylor stood up and looked in amazement at their new allies.

"Do you know where Erdogan is?"

"No," Sarik replied quickly, "but I can find out."

Taylor froze as he heard the words that were like music to his ears.

"How?" he asked urgently, "How quickly?"

"A day, maybe."

"Anything you need is yours. Just find him."

"You wish to kill Erdogan and to take his throne?"

Taylor nodded.

"Many have tried. None have survived."

"It's the only way to end this war."

"If you wish to win, yes."

"You seem pretty certain?"

"If you cannot change something in the course of this next week, you will lose."

"You seem pretty sure on that?" King asked, strolling up to Taylor.

"Erdogan's jump gateway is days from completion, and should you present any chance of winning, and even if you can stop it, Lord Erdogan will not let you have this world. He would rather see it burn than for you to seize it from him."

"What are you saying?"

"The Kiyamet."

Taylor could see Jafar knew exactly what Sarik was speaking of.

"Erdogan would not destroy this paradise world," Jafar insisted.

"If the choice was to destroy it or concede to Colonel Taylor and the rest of the humans, yes he would."

"What the hell is this Kiyamet?"

"A device buried deep below the surface of a world. When activated, it will systematically destroy the atmosphere so that nothing living can survive. Whatever planet is struck by the Kiyamet is uninhabitable for thousands of years."

"And he's building one of these things here?" Taylor asked.

"It is already built and ready to be activated."

Taylor's face went white as he considered the prospect of the weapon being activated.

"Scorched Earth? Just like Demiran tried?" King asked.

"I thought Erdogan was above such tantrums?" Morris said.

"Pride," said Silva, "He doesn't believe he can lose, and this way he wins no matter which way it goes."

Taylor thought about everything he was hearing. He wanted to take it to the commanders of their forces and fleet, but he knew what had to be done, and that he had to be the one to do it. He turned back to Sarik.

"Whatever you have to do, find him. Twenty-four hours, that's all you've got."

Sarik nodded and turned to leave.

"Where are you going?" Irala asked him.

He stopped and turned back around in surprise.

"I cannot find him here. I will take ten of my people and discover his location."

Irala looked to Taylor for him to intervene.

"What? We either trust them or we don't."

He could see that no one trusted them, and he doubted the decision himself but knew it was their best, and probably only hope. Sarik looked to him for approval, and so he inclined his head and watched his latest ally leave.

"You can't be serious?" Morris asked, "You know they can't be trusted, and the first thing you do is give them this much responsibility? First thing they'll probably do is to tell Erdogan where you are. You know how much Erdogan wants to see you dead?"

Taylor agreed, but he was soon distracted by the realisation that he was the greatest bait of them all.

"How many of us do they have to kill before you realise they cannot be our friends?" Morris asked after he didn't get an answer to his initial questions. Taylor merely pointed to Jafar.

"You know how many times that alien has saved my life?" Taylor whispered, "You know how much he has done for our cause? More than you ever have or ever can hope to. Don't like trusting someone new? Join the club. Present me with a better idea, and I'll think about it."

Morris said nothing, and Taylor moved back to King.

"We're holding here. Secure the area."

King nodded and didn't even attempt to question the orders. Taylor gestured for Jafar to walk with him, and he took a few paces away from the group that was hanging on to his ever word.

"Do you think I can trust this Sarik?" Taylor asked quietly.

"I do not know. He appears honourable, but we will not know where his loyalties lie until we see proof."

"That's a big help."

Jafar said nothing.

Several hours had passed, and the sun was low in the sky. They had seen no enemy presence or attempts to retaliate, as they would have expected. Taylor sat on the rooftop of an apartment building in the city centre and was just staring up into the sky. The stars were becoming visible. He wanted nothing more than to have Eli at his side. Finally, it was his comms bleeper than interrupted his dream, and he activated the video display. A screen projected before him. It was the bridge of the Diderot, with White and Lasure looking in at him.

"Colonel Taylor, we are glad to hear of your successful operation in Warsaw, but we have been informed that you have recruited enemy forces. And not only that, but that you have set them free to act at their own will," said Lasure.

"Not their own will," he replied.

"...And that you have been withholding vital information from us," White added.

He got up and walked to the edge of the rooftop and took a deep breath as they waited for him to go on.

"I have a question for you both, and I'm guessing you understand now that this situation is far more serious than we thought. Do you want Erdogan dead?"

"Of course, but…"

"But nothing," Taylor interrupted, "He has eluded us all this time. We keep pushing, and it'll be the end of us all. But there is one thing I can guarantee he wants just as much as this world…me."

"What are you saying, Colonel?" General White asked.

"If we keep pursing Erdogan, we will lose. He has outsmarted us at every stage, and any sizeable operation to track him down he will see through every time. I want to go in, as bait."

"Alone?" Lasure gasped.

"Sarik, the alien officer I freed, I believe he can get me to Erdogan, along with a few of my people."

"It's suicide."

"No, General, to carry on with our current course of action is suicide. I am sure Morris has already informed you of this doomsday weapon Erdogan has installed on our planet. We can't win this through conventional war."

"Going after Erdogan like this, you won't survive it."

"No, probably not, Admiral."

"And you think you can beat him?"

"I have a fighter's chance, and it's a damn sight better than anything else we can do."

All of them went quiet for a moment, thinking over what he had said. White broke the silence.

"Has it really come to this? Is our only hope left in a

handful of men throwing themselves into the hands of the enemy, and hoping to kill him by some miracle? After everything, is that what it comes down to?"

"It's that simple, yes," replied Taylor, "I have a chance at this, and whether you accept it or not, I am going to give it a shot."

"You've accepted you might not come back from this, but what of the men and women you expect to go with you?"

"They know as well as I do, General, that without this it is all over anyway. They'll stand with me until the end."

"Okay," Lasure finally conceded, "I don't like it, but I guess we have no choice but to give it a shot. What can we do?"

"Just keep doing what you're doing. Attack ground targets and put pressure on the enemy, but not so much that Erdogan presses the button. Other than that, leave it to me."

"If what this alien has told you is right, you're our only hope," added White.

"And if he lies and is drawing you into a trap, we will lose more than we could ever afford to."

"Admiral, it's not over until I kill that bastard. It doesn't matter what it costs, I will not be done in this life until he is dead."

"You have our approval, Colonel," said Lasure, "and we will do as you ask. Good luck."

Taylor ended the transmission.

He looked up at the sun casting its final rays on the hills in the distance, and he revelled in the peace and tranquillity that the night would bring.

"So it's all on us?" King asked.

Taylor turned in surprise as he had thought he was alone.

"I've got to do this, and I won't ask any one of you to come with me. Any man or woman who goes down this road does so of their own free will."

"Come on, Taylor, don't give me that shit. Save those speeches for the rest of the Regiment, you don't need to convince me. I know what needs to be done in this war. I knew the day it started. I knew what had to be done the day we disobeyed orders and flew to Europe to save your ass, and we did."

"Yeah, you did," replied Taylor with a slight chuckle, "You were our guardian angels that day."

"Still are. You're a credit to the Corps, Colonel, but you needed the Rangers to carry you."

That remark made Taylor laugh out loud for the first time in a long while. He turned and leaned over the ledge and looked down into the street. King joined him. They could see a few dozen of their own and almost as many of the Sampions.

"Look at us," said King, "We're the most ridiculous make up of a regiment that ever existed. We've got people from a dozen nations and services, and fucking aliens. Aliens? You know how crazy that would have sounded a few years ago?"

Taylor smiled.

"It's crazy, and it shouldn't work, but it does, because at the heart of it we have you holding it all together. I don't know what great creator or God chose you, but you were always destined to end this war," said King.

"Fate?" Taylor asked, "I don't believe in it."

"Yeah, well suck it up, because she believes in you. The things you've been through, the things you've achieved. No human could have done it. With crazy luck, you might have achieved a quarter of what you have, but not this. You were born for this, and I'm honoured to walk beside you to the very end of whatever destiny was laid down for you."

Taylor shook his head and smiled again. He still couldn't accept than anything was predetermined, but there was no denying that he should have been killed many times over.

"Think they'll come back?" Taylor asked to shift the subject matter.

"Sarik?"

Taylor nodded.

"Oh, they'll come back all right. Only question is do they come alone or with a whole fucking army to run us into the ground?"

"Guess we'll just have to wait and see, then, Captain."

He already doubted his decisions and their new allies, but was well aware he could not show it.

"Get some rest," he added, "One way or another, we're gonna need it for tomorrow."

Taylor took on his own advice and bed down for the night. He had a restless hour as thoughts rolled around his head, but finally his exhaustion overcame his worry. He snapped out of his sleep when he found someone shaking him and awoke to find that it was Corporal Herrera.

"Sorry, Sir, but Sarik has returned."

"With what?"

Herrera look confused.

"What he left with, Sir."

Taylor leapt up and grabbed his rifle. He had fallen asleep in full combat gear, having only removed his helmet that he picked up from the floor nearby. He rushed out of the building and found Sarik awaiting him with two-dozen of his own troops.

"Have you found him?" Taylor asked breathlessly upon spotting the alien.

"Yes."

Taylor stopped and froze. He couldn't believe what he was hearing.

"Where is he?" King asked. He'd rushed up beside them.

"Brest."

"Shit, that's not far from here," replied King.

"Does he have any inclination that you are fighting for us?" Taylor asked.

Sarik shook his head.

"I would not have returned if that were the case," he replied.

"All right, options. Can you nuke it from orbit?"

Sarik shook his head.

"Brest is one of the greatest fortresses I have ever seen. Aerial defence platforms would destroy anything from the air, and even your nuclear weapons would have little effect against its surface."

"Ground attack?" King asked.

"In time it could succeed, with enough resources, but Erdogan would escape long before that could happen."

"How?"

"Erdogan is a wise leader. He has secret exists constructed into every one of his fortresses. With any warning, he can escape before they can be overcome."

"So what are we left with?" Morris joined in with the questions.

King looked to Taylor, and they both knew what had to be done.

"If we cannot corner Erdogan with force, then we will have to do it with cunning," said Taylor.

He caught a glimpse of movement. Kelly and Becker were approaching, and with several of their Company at their backs.

"I thought it was bullshit when I heard you'd sided with them," said Kelly, "Now I see it's true, and I wonder if the world hasn't turned upside down, Colonel."

"Easy now, Kelly. These guys are with us," said Taylor.

Kelly looked at the aliens from head to toe and then back to Taylor for confirmation.

"You trust them?" he asked.

Taylor nodded.

"Then so do I, until they give me reason to think otherwise."

Taylor nodded once again in appreciation of his understanding, although he also accepted how bizarre a situation it was.

"Sarik, can you get close to Erdogan?"

"I believe so."

"And can you kill him?"

Sarik shook his head.

"No."

"Why the hell not?" King shouted.

"Not through choice," added Sarik, "Erdogan is the greatest of us all. None have ever defeated him, even in friendly contest and sport."

"And I can't beat him either," Taylor said, "I faced him once, and he is a formidable foe, but I don't intend to fight him alone!"

"If you wish to defeat Erdogan, and take his position, he must be beaten in single combat for you to gain the respect and power of his armies," Sarik said.

"What happens and what we report don't have to be the same thing, though, do they? Let's worry about killing the bastard first."

Many shook their heads in disbelief and astonishment.

"I know this is crazy!" Taylor said, "but this whole damn war is crazy!"

He paced up and down as he thought it over, and finally turned to Sarik.

"You can definitely get close to Erdogan?"

The alien nodded.

"How many of your own Sampions can you get there to support you?"

"Not many, maybe one or two."

"Not enough," muttered Taylor, "How many of us could you get in the same room as him, as your prisoners?"

"Maybe ten, if they were your finest, and he believed they could be valuable trophies."

Taylor paced up and down, trying to piece together a plan of action. When he stopped, almost a hundred of those under his command were now waiting for his response.

"Then this is what we will do. We will give Erdogan exactly what he wants. Myself, and my best fighters and closest friends."

It was a terrifying notion that no one was able to respond to.

"Desperate times call for desperate measures!" he shouted and strode up to Sarik.

"Will you take us as your prisoners, and will you support us when the time comes?"

"Yes."

"I will not ask any one of you to come along with me on this, and I can almost guarantee that those who go will not survive! Erdogan has to believe this is real, my closest friends and comrades. Which of you will follow me and see this through?"

Kelly stepped forward immediately and without hesitation.

"I will!" he said proudly.

Taylor was surprised, but he could not turn away his friend. He looked to King who nodded back, looking into his eyes. Silva stepped forward a second later and raised his artificial hand in a fist.

"With you to the end, Colonel," he stated.

The offers continued to flood in thick and fast, and he soon realised he would have to pick and choose, as ten times the number he needed volunteered. He paced up and down again and finally stopped to make his decision.

"Kelly, King, Silva, Herrera, Lang, Matthews, Williams, Ryan, Pitt!" he called.

He knew there was still one to be called. He looked around the group that had amassed around him. Becker stood behind Kelly, but looked down and away, he was glad of it. The German tank commander had seen enough bloodshed, and he was not the man for the job. Morris did not volunteer, and he thought no lesser of him for it, but then he noticed Captain Reynolds nudging Kelly.

"May I suggest Captain Reynolds," stated Kelly.

Taylor knew little of the man and wasn't sure, but Kelly's recommendation sealed the deal.

"Reynolds it is!" replied Taylor as he turned back to Sarik.

"I assume you can get Jafar in disguised as one of your own?"

"Yes, that is possible," said Sarik.

"Then it is decided. When can we go?"

"As soon as you are ready."

"No time like the now," said Taylor, "How do we do this?"

"Come with us, and we will take you to Erdogan."

The proposal sent a chill down Taylor's spine, but he knew it had to be done. He looked over to his volunteers. They all looked just as ready and terrified in equal measure as he felt deep down. Irala appeared beside him.

"Colonel Taylor, I cannot recommend this course of action, and neither can I assist you with it."

Taylor slowly nodded to him.

"You've done more for us that we could ever have dreamed possible," he replied.

"Colonel Taylor," a voice over his comms.

"This is Taylor," he replied.

"Taylor, we've got a problem."

He recognised the voice now as that of Admiral Lasure. *Oh shit,* he thought.

"This for my ears only?" he asked.

"That would be your decision, but those with you may want and need to hear this."

Taylor pressed a few keys, and a screen projected out before them, showing the Admiral on the bridge of the Diderot.

"Go on," added Taylor.

"Just two minutes ago we received confirmation that a gateway has been established in our Solar System. It appears that it materialised just moments before, and that it is now operational."

"My God," said Kelly, "they've got access to and from their worlds any time they please."

"Yes, as we speak the number of vessels passing through the gateway is increasing in every moment, and they are heading our way."

"Do you have any ability to destroy it?"

Lasure shook his head. "This fleet is far beyond what we are able to handle."

"How long do we have?" Taylor asked.

"Many of the vessels have remained at the gateway, presumably to protect it. Another twenty minutes, and they will have all they need to come right at us."

"So how long can you give us, Admiral?"

"We can hold them here for a little while, but not long. We have perhaps three hours at the most until they're through us and coming for you."

"We could still leave, run like you did before," added Kelly.

They all looked to Taylor for an answer, and he was already shaking his head.

"We don't run," he quickly replied, "We've still got a chance here. We run, and we're on the run for the rest of our miserable existence, but neither will I throw away the lives of everyone here. A handful of us have the chance to do this. Lasure, I want you to hold out as long as you can. Buy us some time and make it look like we're still in this fight, but don't risk anymore than you have to. Get us two hours. That's all I ask."

"We can do that, Colonel. Good luck to you and all those brave people who go with you. You'll have to forgive me, but I have work to do, just as you do."

"Thank you, Admiral, and good luck to you," replied Taylor, and the communication abruptly ended.

He turned to Sarik, "Ready when you are."

The alien immediately led him and the other volunteers onwards. He began to wonder about the alien's motivations now, so he turned to Jafar for answers.

"They can see we're on our last legs, and still they work with us? What do you think is keeping them on our side?"

"Honour," Jafar replied confidently.

"And you don't think he'd forgo that to side with whoever is going to win?"

"Depends how honourable he is."

Taylor sighed as he realised he wasn't going to get a useful answer.

The whole of the Inter-Allied Regiment watched as Taylor, the human volunteers, and Jafar followed their newly discovered allies up a ramp and into their vessel nearby. They were all aboard, and Taylor looked out for one last time through the closing ramped, and he saw Anders take a step forward.

"Go get him, Colonel!" he yelled at the top of his voice.

The rest of the troops erupted into a frenzy as they shouted and hollered all manner of things to give him a proper send off. The door came to a close, and they could hear the engines fire up on the craft.

"Think this was a good idea?" he asked Kelly.

"No," Kelly replied without any hesitation, "but it's a damn sight better than anything else I have heard."

They lifted off the ground and soared into the sky. Taylor glanced over to the cockpit and the alien pilot who flew them. It didn't feel right to be making their last mission without Eddie Rains at the helm, but he was glad the Lieutenant was going to live, as he doubted any of them would.

The aircraft was a tight fit for the twelve of them and

the twenty aliens they travelled with. He turned to Sarik and asked him, "What now?"

"You must hand over your weapons."

"Whoa, hang on!" Kelly shouted, "Ain't no way we're…"

But Taylor raised his hand to call for silence and allowed Saric to go on.

"I can get you into Erdogan's bunker, but only as my prisoners. You must relinquish your weapons."

Taylor looked around and could see his people clutching their weapons close.

"Do as he says!" he ordered.

He put his shield down against the bulkhead and passed his rifle to Sarik. The alien took it and placed it in a storage box beside them, and then turned back and pointed to his side arms. Taylor obliged with a groan, as he could not bear to give it all up. He looked to his own people and gestured for them to do the same. He felt naked now and knew it was the real test of Sarik's loyalty.

"Good luck," said Sarik.

Without any warning at all, the alien lurched forward and drove its armoured fist into his face with all its force. He felt the pain of the impact for just a split second and then his legs gave way as he lost consciousness.

CHAPTER THIRTEEN

Taylor awoke and found himself in almost complete darkness. His arms were restrained at shoulder height. He looked down to his feet, and they were bound also. He was detained in an upright position on some kind of trolley. He looked to one side; Silva was beside him and Lang the other.

"What? Where the hell are we?" he asked.

He couldn't make out anything more of their surroundings in the darkness.

"Told you they couldn't be trusted," said Kelly.

Taylor could hear the voice behind him, but he couldn't see where Kelly was. He said nothing in response. A few seconds later some lights came on and almost blinded them after their eyes had become accustomed to the darkness. They slowly adjusted, and Taylor could see they were in a room only about ten metres square. He could just arch his neck far enough to see Kelly and several of the others on another similar rack nearby. The boxes their equipment had been placed in aboard Sarik's ship stood in one corner.

"Shit me," stated Silva.

"We're really finished now, aren't we?" Herrera said, "Survived all these years, just to be fed to the enemy as a treat."

"It's not over yet," replied Taylor confidently, "While we're still breathing, it isn't over."

Herrera looked at the solid steel shackles that held them in place. They were still wearing their Reitech suits, and yet their power would do nothing to shift the restraints.

"Why, oh why did we ever trust an alien?"

"Cut it out, Kelly!" Taylor shouted, "If it wasn't for some aliens we know, we'd never have made it this far."

"And if it hadn't been for their arrival in the first place, we'd have nothing to worry about, anyway," Kelly spat in anger.

Taylor looked at his watch, but it had been smashed, presumably from when he fell from Sarik's strike.

"How long have I been out?"

"Over ninety minutes," replied Silva.

Taylor thought desperately of something to say or do, but he soon accepted that he was powerless to act.

"Why capture us alive?" he asked himself.

Several of them heard, but nobody responded.

"There's no reason to keep us alive as trophies. We'd be just as good dead. Only reason would be to showcase us, to humiliate us. Erdogan! Where are you? You coward! Come here and fight me yourself!"

Just as his echo ended, a door opened on his side of the room, and Sarik stepped in with three other alien warriors similarly equipped. Gone was his white armour, and back to the black and runes of Erdogan's loyal army.

"You bastard," Taylor sneered, "For all your bullshit about honour, you are just as much the scumbag as your master."

Sarik said nothing as he stepped aside, and a towering figure stepped in through the doorway. It was Erdogan himself. He was fully armoured as if for combat in his finest armour. He stopped and placed a hand onto Sarik's shoulder.

"Well done, you will be rewarded many times over," Erdogan said.

Taylor was more interested in the physical touch. It was all the evidence he needed to know that this was in fact the real Erdogan, and not another hologram. He wasn't sure if that was reassuring or terrifying.

"Colonel Taylor," stated Erdogan in his deep and droning voice, "We were always destined to meet again."

"Yes, you're right about that, and I'm destined to kill you."

Erdogan smiled with a wicked grin. He turned and

paced over to the boxes of their equipment and opened one of the lids. He reached in, pulled out an Assegai, and walked back over to Taylor.

"It would be a lie to say I am not impressed with all that you have achieved. For such a weak race, none have ever provided so much of a challenge in war, and I thank you for that."

"You won't be thanking me when I ram one of those down your throat!" Taylor spat back.

Erdogan grinned once again before firing up the Assegai and moving it in towards him. He was powerless to act, and the creature just placed the very tip onto Taylor's face beside his eye socket and slid it down his cheek. A deep cut was burnt into his face. Taylor clenched his fists and took the pain without making any sound at all.

"Where does this strength come from?" Erdogan questioned.

"You have no idea how strong the human race really is, and it will be the end of you."

Erdogan laughed. It was a deep and booming sound that echoed around the room for several seconds after he'd finished.

"You would like your chance, wouldn't you? Although you failed miserably last time we met, even now, you'd still give anything to fight against me, would you not?"

"Damn right I would."

"And I am going to give it to you," he replied with a

wicked grin.

Taylor's heart sunk. He knew he could not defeat the alien Lord. He looked defiantly into the alien's eyes and didn't show a single ounce of fear, but he felt it deep down inside his very being.

"Yes, you will have your big chance. The one you have always wanted, and you will get it before both my people and yours," he replied and laughed once again.

Taylor could see he was revelling in it. He looked over to Sarik, but the traitor looked away, almost as if in shame.

"That's right. You have no one to turn to any longer," he added.

A screen appeared and projected the full width of the wall in front of Taylor. It was the battle unfolding in space. He could see Lasure's fleet was vastly outnumbered, with ever more enemy ships joining the battle, and yet they fought on. At the very centre, he could see the Diderot receiving a pounding from pulse fire, and still returning as much against it. Fighters ducked and weaved through the friendly fleet and were pursued by squadrons of friendly craft. But for all the valiant effort, he could see they were fighting a losing battle, and yet Lasure would not give up. It was clear to all that they would have jumped out by now if they had any intention of doing so.

"You see the last hope of the human race. How could you ever have stood against me? How could you ever have defeated me?"

"Came pretty close," snapped Taylor.

Erdogan smiled in response, but Taylor could see there was some concern in his eyes. He knew very well that it hadn't been such a clean-cut victory.

"Your world is mine. Soon your fleet will be destroyed, and I will end those wretches who supported you, and all those they now shelter. All that remains is you. The great Colonel Mitch Taylor, saviour of humanity, it is time for the entire Galaxy to see just how weak you really are."

As his final words were spoken, the restraints on Taylor released, and he stepped out before Erdogan. He dared not make a move; he was still unarmed. He took just a single pace out from beside his comrades.

"You want to fight me?" Taylor asked.

"Of course. You have bested Lords of my worlds. Now I must end you in personal combat and forever cement your position as an inferior being in our history."

Taylor wanted to feel positive about the prospect, but he still knew that he could not win.

"Give me my weapons, and I'll gladly end your life," he said defiantly.

Erdogan laughed.

"You may think of this as a fight, if that would please your feeble mind, but this is nothing more than an execution."

"Give me my weapons, now!"

But Erdogan remained calm.

"You will die soon enough, Colonel. You need not rush the experience. I, for one, would wish to prolong this pleasure for as long as may be possible."

He looked down at some display on his forearm and appeared to be miming a count until finally he looked up at Taylor.

"Now it is your time to die."

Not exactly delayed gratification, Taylor thought.

He began to hear the grinding of mechanisms, and the roof above them separated and opened up, revealing the light of day. A few seconds later the floor of what they thought was a room began to rise towards the surface. Taylor was lost for words now. He knew his end was coming, and he resigned himself to dying well, for he was not willing to give Erdogan the satisfaction of an easy victory.

One drop of your blood spilled, and I will die content.

Though even as he said it to himself, he realised that was not true. Deep down he didn't want to die. Not because he hadn't accepted it as necessary, but because he had not accomplished his mission yet. He couldn't bear to die without knowing they had won. He tried to think of some way of getting out of the situation, but he looked around at the faces of his friends and could see there was no hope. Then he realised Jafar was not among them. He wanted to pose the question but stayed silent, in the forlorn hope that his friend may yet come to their aid;

although he knew it was more likely that he was already dead.

The elevator moved slowly towards the surface. So slow in fact that it seemed deliberate to draw out his pain or suffering, or perhaps to stoke Erdogan's ego. At last the surface reached eye level, and Taylor was able see out. He recognised it well, the stadium in France that had been one of his many arenas when he fought the aliens for sport and show.

He began to wonder if the fortress at Brest ever existed, or the alien's apocalyptic weapon that Sarik had revealed to them. He had always known that his fate remained in France. The wars for him were forever tied to that place and appeared to be the hub of the conflict for him.

The stadium was filled, every single seat, and the crowd were roaring with excitement. He turned to look at them all and suddenly stopped. He noticed a section was filled with humans.

"You see, Colonel, this glory will be witnessed by my people, and by yours," said Erdogan.

Tens of thousands of aliens and humans watched, but only the aliens cheered. He could just make out a few of the human faces, and they were distressed enough that he could tell they really were his people, and not Erdogan's clones. The elevator came to a stop as it reached the surface, and Erdogan stepped out. He raised his arms to play to the crowd, and their volume only increased with sheer ecstasy.

He stopped and turned back to look at Taylor. He was still standing beside his comrades that remained detained.

"Where are your friends now? Unable to help you. Unable to save you. You cannot hide behind them anymore. Nor can you hide behind the protection of your traitorous dog and the Aranui who will soon be dust beneath my feet!"

The voice carried throughout the stadium through some hidden microphones and speakers that ensured every soul in the audience got a front row seat to their confrontation. Taylor shook his head. The alien disgusted and repulsed him, and he knew that all that was left was to save face before his death.

"You talk big for someone who thinks he is all powerful. You have something to prove?"

The crowd fell silent, and Erdogan looked far from pleased. He stormed over to a crate nearby and pulled out a huge two-handed sword. The blade was lightly curved and sharp along its front edge and twenty centimetres of the back edge. The grip recurved in the opposite direction to the blade. A bowl guard protected the lead hand and swirling bars out around much of the grip to extend its protection. Bronze and gold runes glimmered along the blade's length, and the spine of the single edged blade was blued. The pommel flowed seamlessly in shape from the grip much like a knife, and as cut from a bright crystal that appeared as a diamond.

"I could have killed every one of your friends before you! But better still, I want them to see the demise of the great Colonel Taylor, and I want them to live out their lives as slaves with this memory burnt into their eyes!"

Taylor finally smiled. It pleased him that he was striking Erdogan at the core. His defiance was the last card he had to play.

"Give him his weapons!" Erdogan ordered.

Sarik opened one of the crates near the prisoners and pulled out a shield and an Assegai.

"Your weapons that you hold so dear. Let's see how they fare against a real opponent," added Erdogan.

Sarik walked to Taylor and passed him his weapons by hand when he had expected them to be thrown before him. Sarik leaned in close as he handed them over.

"Keep him distracted," he whispered.

Taylor didn't know how to take the statement, but he took his weapons without hesitation as Sarik quickly stepped away and out of his reach. He squared off against Erdogan in the centre of the arena and looked back to Sarik one last time. The creature did nothing, not a single sign of acknowledgement.

Taylor let out a roar and rushed forward without any hesitation at all. He charged towards the towering alien leader, who stood his ground confidently and raised his blade in two hands. Taylor went forward with his shield held high and tried to barge the alien, but Erdogan nimbly leapt aside to Taylor's left, but no made no attempt to strike him.

Erdogan laughed as he stepped and that only infuriated Taylor. He rushed forward again, and once more Erdogan attempted to leap to the blind side of his shield. This time Taylor swung the shield wide and clipped Erdogan with the edge. The impact knocked Erdogan off balance as he was moving, and he stumbled a few paces before regaining his balance. Taylor turned and smiled at the embarrassment, but he knew the punishment would be severe.

The alien Lord stormed angrily forward now and swung a strong but well controlled vertical cut for Taylor, who narrowly avoided it. The blade struck the ground beside him, but before he could respond, Erdogan swung a back edge cut that smashed into his shield and launched him off his feet. He hit the ground hard and felt the back of his helmet smash into the ground. He looked at his shield; a deep groove had been pressed in with the thick back edge of Erdogan's sword. He knew that if that was what the blunt edge could do, he was in trouble.

Erdogan seemed to be too keen pandering to the crowd to worry about finishing him off. He got back up to his feet slowly and took in a deep breath as he tried to find some way of approaching his deadly opponent, but his time to plan was soon lost as the creature strode confidently towards him. Taylor backed off a few paces and then side stepped as he tried to step under Erdogan's blade, but it struck the top corner of his shield and sliced off a triangle of it without meeting much resistance at all.

Taylor's eyes caught Sarik's as he noticed the creature nod intentionally at him. He knew he had nothing to lose and decided on a course of action to put Erdogan's back against Sarik and his friends to see if the turncoat really was still on his side.

"Taylor! Taylor! Taylor!" the voices chanted from the human prisoners in the audience.

The chant was getting louder, and it seemed to infuriate Erdogan further.

"Come on, you bastard!" Taylor shouted.

He rushed ahead and thrust towards Erdogan before he could swing. The alien parried his strike off to one side with the long grip of his sword between his two hands. He followed it with a diagonal cut, but Taylor managed to place his shield at an acute angle that deflected it. He drove his shield forward and smashed it into Erdogan and forced him backwards. As the alien staggered back, Taylor rushed at him and deliberately smashed his one side that caused him to turn, but Erdogan struck him with the pommel of his sword to his face as he stormed past.

The blow struck like a sledgehammer to Taylor's face, and he felt two of his teeth break free and blood poured out from his mouth. He turned and dropped to one knee in agony, but he soon looked up defiantly at Erdogan who was looking down and marvelling at his work. Taylor turned his attention to what was now going on behind the alien Lord. He could see one of the guards near the detainment rack press a few buttons, and the shackles of Kelly and all who were with him became free. The alien's helmet folded back into itself to reveal Jafar.

Erdogan turned just in time to see Sarik release the prisoners on the other block. The two remaining alien guards lay dead.

"What are you doing?" he boomed.

"Following a wiser leader," replied Sarik.

Erdogan turned back to Taylor, and it was clear that he was furious.

"What's the matter, things not going quite to plan?" Taylor asked, as blood still dripped from his mouth.

Erdogan let out a cry of anger and ran at Sarik. He swung a heavy blow that cut through the glaive that he was carrying and drove him back. Sarik fought back with the two remaining pieces of his weapon in each hand. He smashed the pole into Erdogan's arm and tried to hit him again, but Erdogan drove his pommel upwards and knocked Sarik off his feet.

"Get your weapons!" Taylor shouted to his friends.

They didn't hesitate to rush to the crates. Silva drew out his assault rifle and quickly fired a few shots into Erdogan's flank, but the shots glanced off his armour. The alien barely even seemed to notice the impacts and continued on against Sarik, who raised his arm to parry a cut from the ground. Erdogan smashed his weapon down and then cut again. The powerful blow took Sarik's right arm off at the elbow.

Their alien ally screamed out in agony. Blood poured out across the arena, and the crowd roared with excitement. Erdogan raised his sword in both hands above his head for a brutal cut that would have ended Sarik, but as he brought it down, he felt an impact in his side. Taylor smashed into him and launched him off his feet. The two landed clumsily on the arena surface; a hard and fine gravel that kicked up dust.

Taylor tried to thrust into Erdogan, but he was met with an elbow that connected with immense force to his head. He rolled out of the way and both got to their feet. Erdogan froze now as he looked around. He was now encircled by Taylor's Inter-Allied force. Twelve opponents.

He looked to the audience, and not one of them came forward to help. It was clear to him they expected him to win, no matter what. He looked back to Jafar.

"You can't really be for these humans? Come back to me now, and stand as my champion and have everything you ever wished for."

Taylor smiled, knowing the alien was showing fear now.

"You walked this path. You asked for this," replied Taylor, "Your vanity brought you to this point, your arrogance. For all that you are, you are no better a man than Demiran or Karadag before you."

"You will swallow those words," he replied venomously.

"Go forward together!" Taylor called out, "Just as we trained, maximise our numbers, and keep your head on your shoulders!"

He advanced first, and the others quickly closed to box Erdogan in, but none of them were under any illusions that the creature didn't still posed an immense threat. As they closed in, Erdogan raised his sword as if to strike Taylor, and then swung it in a broad horizontal stroke that caused most to leap back as the blade carved into several shields. In the confusion, the enemy Lord leapt forward at King. The immense pace caught him off guard, and the alien's blade cut down deep into the top edge of his shield and drove down into his left collar.

King winced in pain but still thrust forward with his Assegai. Erdogan kicked the blade down and swung for his head, but the impact was displaced by Lang's shield. The German thrust inwards, and Erdogan parried, but Reynolds drove his Assegai into his flank. He got just a few centimetres in when the creature snapped around and swung a heavy horizontal strike with his sword. The blade sliced through Reynolds' neck and took his head off in one.

Erdogan backed off and looked cautiously around him as they circled him once more. Kelly looked down at his fallen friend for just a second, but he knew he could not afford to any longer. Kelly jumped forward, but he was slow compared to the younger fighters. Erdogan backed off from a strike and kicked him back before turning to Pitt. He grabbed the Private's shield and tore it down before thrusting his sword through his mouth so that it pierced through the back of his skull. But Erdogan did not draw the blade out. He simply pulled sideways and cut out from the man's head.

Silva was on him next and thrust forward before Pitt's body had even hit the ground. Erdogan parried the strike, just as Kelly smashed the lower edge of his shield into the back of Erdogan's leg and drove him down onto one knee. Silva's Assegai was descending towards Erdogan's chest with a downward thrust when the creature reached up with its left hand and grabbed hold of Silva, stopping him dead. He stood up and threw the Sergeant Major, cutting at him as he did. The cut drove several centimetres past his armour and into his ribs.

Silva landed on Williams who broke his fall, but he was in agony.

"Close in on him!" Taylor screamed.

The creature darted off to one side again to engage Matthews and swung a cut towards his head, but at the last moment redirected and cut across his legs, cutting both limbs at the thighs. Matthews screamed out in pain as the blood gushed, and it was clear he would be dead in minutes if not seconds.

Jafar and Taylor leapt forward to try and close in on Erdogan who was now going for Williams. The Private was backing off and not standing as Taylor had told him. Erdogan was able to get him alone and cut once that struck his shield in half. His second strike cut through the Private's Assegai and sliced deep into his collar and killed him instantly.

The circle closed in on Erdogan once again, and Jafar went forward. He ducked under a cut and thrust up with his Assegai. The strike was quick and precise but only scraped Erdogan's armour as he voided away, but he was met with the edge of Taylor's shield that crashed into his face. Taylor quickly made use of his opportunity and drove his Assegai into Erdogan's stomach. The blade went twenty centimetres in when the creature grasped his hand and stopped it going any further. He drew out the blade and smashed an elbow into Taylor's head, and then cut down towards his head with his mightier sword.

Ryan pushed his shield in between the weapon and Taylor just in time, but the sword cut through the lower half of his shield and through Taylor's also until embedding into Taylor's armour and cutting a centimetre deep into his left arm. Silva struck the sword with the edge of his shield, and the sword was knocked out of the alien's grasp. He immediately struck a back fist to Silva's face then smashed him to the ground and stunned him for a moment.

Erdogan then leapt onto Ryan and put both hands

around his helmet and snapped his neck. Herrera swung for Erdogan, but the alien leapt into a roll and picked up his sword as he nimbly landed back on his feet and thrust it through Lang's shield. The point pierced his chest and heart, and Erdogan drew it out slowly with glee as the body dropped before him.

The circle formed once again, only half of the number they had started with. Taylor could see blue blood seeping from the two wounds on Erdogan. His movement had slowed just a little now, but it didn't seem enough to stop him.

"Little humans, how could you ever have beaten me?" he asked.

"You're going down, and you're going down on live TV for all your people to see," replied Taylor.

Kelly lurched forward first, but Erdogan cut across with a quick slash that sliced his cheek and through his lip and down to his chin. He recoiled back in pain as Silva passed him once again, despite his wound. He pushed his shield up and under Erdogan and tried to thrust, but Erdogan drove his pommel down with both hands onto the shield, and that smashed his shield down. Herrera was quick to attack beside him and thrust the tip of his Assegai into Erdogan's thigh.

The alien let out a scream of agony before cutting Herrera's shield in half and forcing the blade deep into his arm. He drew out the blade and cut around and drove the blade so deep into the Corporal's collar that it drove halfway down his lungs and killed him instantly.

Taylor passed under the blade and smashed his shield into Erdogan's jaw and then thrust for his chest again, but Erdogan parried the strike and spun and delivered a wicked cut into Taylor's flank. The blade drove deep through his ribs, and Taylor dropped to his knees as he felt his legs give out. Erdogan quickly pulled the blade out and cut for his collar as he had done to Herrera. Taylor fell back in pain, and the cut fell short and just sliced into the side of his neck.

Jafar leapt forwards to stop Erdogan finishing the job. Erdogan spun around and cut his Assegai in half. Jafar continued on anyway, jumped over the blade, and leapt onto Erdogan's back and locked him in a chokehold. Erdogan reached to cut him with his sword, but Kelly drove his Assegai into his lead arm. The beast cried out once again in pain as he dropped the sword. A fifty-centimetre blade darted out from that same arm, and Erdogan cut across Kelly's face and then drove the blade into his shoulder. Kelly dropped his weapon as he felt the feeling in his arm vanish, and he fell down while still impaled.

Sarik appeared amongst them and cut down against Erdogan with what was left of his glaive in the only hand he had left. Erdogan was forced to draw out the blade from Kelly to parry this new attack, and followed it with a quick slash across Sarik's face. A punch from his other hand sent him tumbling to the ground.

Jafar smashed his shield against Erdogan and thrust in for his armpit. The strike landed, but Erdogan stopped the blade with his offhand before it had penetrated more than a few millimetres into his skin. Erdogan turned all his fury and anger on the alien now. He punched him in the centre of the chest with a heavy blow that took the wind out of him. He followed it with a slash that cut into his stomach and another three punches until Jafar was unconscious and lay helpless before him. He was just about to drive his blade into Jafar's head when Taylor yelled out.

"Erdogan!"

The alien lord turned to Taylor to see that across the arena he was being helped to his feet by Silva. King stood beside them also. All three men were exhausted and bloody. They looked as if they could barely stand, and they were all who now opposed him. Taylor was pale and looked like he was almost dead already.

"Let's finish this, Erdogan!"

The alien Lord stepped several paces to his right flank and picked up the massive two-handed blade that he had used to such gruesome effect.

He looked to the other two, and both were as weak and badly hurt. Only King still had his shield.

"We can't win and survive," he whispered to the other two.

It was clear that Erdogan overheard him and smiled

in response. Taylor muttered a few things far quieter and then waited for him to come forward. The three of them stayed close and didn't make a single step as the alien came storming towards them for one last time.

Taylor took a breath of the air. It was putrid from the sweat and blood all around, but he could still taste the freshness of the air that he knew as home. Time slowed now as he carefully studied everything before him. He could see Erdogan analysing his every move and anticipating where he would go. The alien came at him with a thrust that he knew would drive right through him, and he could see Erdogan preparing his second move. But Taylor did not move. He took the thrust square in the chest. The blade drove deep and touched the back plate of his armour. He dropped to his knees and Erdogan in that one moment was frozen in shock.

Silva thrust quickly into the alien's chest and drove the blade home. Erdogan tried to draw the blade out, but Taylor took hold of it in one hand, and his left hand in the other, and pulled himself further onto the blade and so locking his opponent in combat. King thrust his Assegai into Erdogan's flank, and the alien cried out in pain. He let go of his sword with his lead arm and slashed at Silva with his arm-mounted blade. Silva was unable to stop the power of the blow in his weakened state, and it drove down into his neck. Erdogan pulled back the blade, and thrust it into his heart, killing him instantly.

But as he did, Taylor lifted up his Assegai and plunged it down into the chest of Erdogan just below his neck and drove it deep down to the hilt. Erdogan went rigid as the blade struck the internal organs in his body, and he froze as he lost feeling in his spine. Taylor reached for King who helped him to his feet.

The crowd watched in silent amazement as Taylor placed both hands on the blade that had skewed him, and drew it out as blood poured down his armour. Finally, he pulled the blade free. Despite being shaky on his feet, he took the grip in two hands and raised it up over Erdogan's head.

"I told you I'd kill you before this was over, and I never break a promise."

He slashed down with the sword and cleaved the alien's head off with one strike, though the body stayed like a statue before him. He turned and looked out to the crowd to see they were all standing in shock and horror. The humans were clapping and cheering now. Once again they chanted his name, and after a few moments, the alien crowd began to chant it, too.

Taylor's energy was failing, and he was about to fall when King grabbed his one arm, and Kelly staggered over to support his other side.

"We've got to get you a medic now!" King shouted.

Taylor shook his head.

"Too late for that," he whispered, "There is one last

thing I have to do."

He looked over to Sarik. He was helping Jafar up with his one good hand and had somehow cauterised the joint where he had lost his forearm.

"This can be seen by all?" Taylor asked him.

"This is being shown live to everyone on Earth, and transmitted out to the fleet and into our homelands through the gateway," he replied.

He nodded before shaking free of those helping him. He slowly staggered back over to Erdogan's body and lifted up his severed head. He stumbled a few paces as he did so, and Kelly was quick to support him. Taylor lifted up the head to the crowd.

"I have defeated your Lord, and as you as my witnesses, I claim his title, as is my right!"

He coughed out blood as he finished and took in a few deep breaths as he tried to go on.

Kelly wanted to say something, but he could see in Taylor's eyes that he could not.

"As your leader, I am here to tell you that this war is over! There is no winner. The only losers are all those we have lost fighting all these years. This is my first command as your Lord. My second, is that I appoint Jafar, one of your own, to serve in my stead!"

He shouted and gestured towards Jafar for the wounded alien to join them.

"Jafar has served me well, and he is a credit to your

people. This is my decision, and it beyond contestation! There is to be peace!"

Taylor felt his legs go out, and the energy finally leave his body as he fell unconscious.

* * *

"It's been a week already, there must be some change by now?" Kelly demanded.

"There is. Colonel Taylor is deteriorating. He has massive internal organ damage. We have done what we can, but he is dying," replied the Doctor.

"Not good enough. You can't let him die!" Coco said desperately.

They looked in on Taylor who was inside an incubation chamber in intensive care. His life signs were minimal, and there was no sign of him waking up. Twenty of the Inter-Allied were crammed into the room with Coco at their head, and Irala stood beside her.

"Irala, why can't you do something?"

"I am sorry, but we do not have the ability to save your Colonel," he replied.

The Doctor continued, "The Colonel is dying, and there is nothing we can do to stop that."

"Unacceptable," King said, "You have to find a way. You know who he is, and how important he is. You cannot let him die!"

The Doctor shook his head and wiped his brow, and it was clear to King there was something he was holding back.

"Come on, Doc, spit it out," said King.

"Nothing we can do now can save him, and he will die in a matter of days, weeks at the most."

"Okay, so what aren't you telling us?" Kelly asked.

"The only way that Colonel Taylor can be kept alive to put him on ice."

"Cryostasis? Nobody has survived it."

"Not true," replied the Doctor, "Shortly before the first war, a Korean scientist successfully used experimental cryostasis technology. Her patient survived over a one year period, the only one ever."

"One patient?" King muttered. He sounded horrified.

"I didn't say it was a good idea, or one that I would recommend, or is even likely to succeed. But at least with this method, the Colonel has some small chance of life in the future, as opposed to certain death."

"If this works, when can we wake him up?" Coco asked.

The Doctor looked confused.

"We cannot. We do not have the technology to repair the damage done to his body, but future generations may do. Advances take place in medicine and science everyday."

"So we might never see him awake ever again?"

"That is correct, Captain King."

Tears poured down Coco's face, but she looked to King

and Kelly, and both nodded in agreement.

"It's his only chance," Kelly stammered.

* * *

Five years later

Coco stood at the window of a shop in Paris watching a news channel. Her five-year old son grasped her hand and stood beside her mesmerised by the screen. It was Taylor's last battle with Erdogan, heavily edited for the news broadcast. The two of them watched in silence as they listened to the newsreader.

"Today marks five years since the triumphant victory over the Lord Erdogan and marked the first day of the peace that we enjoy today. Above all, that peace must surely be attributed to Colonel Mitch Taylor of the Independent Inter-Allied Regiment. The Colonel's service was colourful and controversial during is career, and today is a clear sign that his legacy lives on to this day. On this fifth anniversary, a statue to this great hero will be unveiled here in Paris, the site of the epic final battle. Colonel Taylor, whose body still remains mortally wounded and in cryostasis, will be interned today at this memorial site, to forever be protected and watched over by local authorities. That is until what some believe will be the day that advances in technology may once again see the Colonel walk among us. We go live shortly, as Colonel

Taylor's cryostasis chamber will be paraded through the streets to a crowd that seems as much in awe and honour of this hero, as others are to protest his arrival and remind us of his darker days."

Coco turned and left the screen. She took a bend to see a police line assembled with lines of fans one side of the road and protestors the other. She paced up to the police line and showed her ID. She was quickly let through. She walked several blocks and finally a statue came into view. Twenty metres tall, the statue in the likeness of Taylor stood atop the stone column. He held the head of Erdogan high in one hand and his Assegai in another, in a pose that appeared stolen from Perseus carrying the head of Medusa.

She was shown through crowds of both humans and Krys supporters until finally she reached the front and found the only face she recognised, Kelly. The scar across his face, mouth, and chin were severe and yet worn with pride.

"Coco, come on," he insisted.

"Thank you," she replied, "Why aren't you with the Regiment?"

He shook his head and smiled, "I was too old for all this when the war began. I have outstayed my welcome. And who is this young chap?"

"Charlie," she replied with a smile.

They heard the volume of voices all around them

increase with excitement, and it was clear that Taylor was approaching. They turned and could see the column coming down the long pathway laid out between the crowds. It took ten minutes for them to reach the statue, and Coco was soon reduced to tears. She watched as the troops of the Inter-Allied carried Taylor inside the thick walled base of the statue that was ten metres wide.

"Do you think he will ever live again?" she asked Kelly.

"Taylor is the most remarkable being I have ever had the privilege of knowing. He will come back to us one day. He seems destined to fight for this world. We may have this peace now, but peace never lasts forever. When he is needed, I am sure he will come back."

They watched the Inter-allied troops lay the chamber down inside the vault of the statue and formed up in front of it. The door shut before them. They each wore the uniforms of the regiments and nations they had come from, and yet they stood together as the force Taylor had made them.

Jafar and Sarik stood off to one side with dozens of Krys representatives. Kelly wrapped an arm around Coco wept uncontrollably.

"He was never going to walk out of this war, was he?" she asked.

Kelly shook his head.

"Taylor was born, bred, and built for that war. His job is done, and we are free and alive. We owe him everything, and maybe one day we will yet be able to thank him. But for now, we can honour him, and do precisely what he fought for. He fought for this world, and our right to live on it. The Battle for Earth is over, and we won."

As the troops retired, Kelly and Coco stepped up to the base of the statue to read the inscription. It read.

'Here lies the living body of Colonel Taylor, Hero of Earth.'